A Christmas Carol

A Christmas Carol

THE ORIGINAL MANUSCRIPT EDITION

CHARLES DICKENS

FOREWORD BY COLM TÓIBÍN

INTRODUCTION BY DECLAN KIELY

PUBLISHED IN ASSOCIATION WITH THE MORGAN LIBRARY & MUSEUM

W. W. NORTON & COMPANY

INDEPENDENT PUBLISHERS SINCE 1923

NEW YORK LONDON

Manufacturing by RR Donnelley Shenzhen
Book design by JAMdesign
Production manager: Julia Druskin

ISBN 978-0-393-60864-9

W. W. Norton & Company, Inc.
500 Fifth Avenue, New York, N.Y. 10110
www.wwnorton.com

W. W. Norton & Company Ltd.
Castle House, 75/76 Wells Street, London W1T 3QT

1 2 3 4 5 6 7 8 9 0

Contents

Foreword

COLM TÓIBÍN

A Christmas Carol takes the form of a dark journey of the soul from willfulness, selfishness, and miserliness toward redemption, happiness, and generosity. The figure of Scrooge is initially presented as a man locked into unhappy solitude and petty cruelty, someone whose ungiving, unyielding, and resolute nature causes him no joy but rather a grim satisfaction at having power over others, a power which he will wield in the darkest days of winter with particular determination, a power which goes against the very idea of what became known as the Christmas spirit.

This idea of Christmas, which the story itself did much to popularize, was already being preached about and written about in newspaper editorials when *A Christmas Carol* appeared in 1843. Christmas, in its new manifestation, would include the idea of giving as well as receiving, of looking after the less fortunate as well as eating well and spending time with family and in good company.

For this reinvention of a tradition to become even more popular, an image was needed of a man who deliberately excluded himself from the cheer and the coziness that the tradition, in all its fragility, implied.

In the story, this man would be taken by ghosts and spirits through a personal purgatory in order to emerge purified. He would see many things that would horrify him or make him feel guilty and unloved, all the more to make the communal cheer of Christmas seem relished by those who had begun to enjoy it. The story takes pleasure in the nightmare visions Scrooge must witness; these horrifying visions, the details of their descriptions, have richer textures than the subsequent images of Scrooge as a man who has learned his lesson and who has resolved to change his life.

Part of the power of the book comes from the grim, unearthly picture its pages draw of London. Since London was a collection of villages in which anyone moving from a posh square to an important public building could catch a glimpse of many side streets which housed the poor, in which privileged and pauper passed each other daily, then the novel itself gained nourishment from the friction between classes, from the closeness of the little streets to the great.

In the later nineteenth century a number of writers saw the startling possibilities such contrasts offered, where the London of Dickens, so sprawling, vast, and filled with drama, could be rendered also as a ghostly place where substance became shadow. In books such as Robert Louis Stevenson's *Strange Case of Dr. Jekyll and Mr. Hyde* (1886) or Oscar Wilde's *The Picture of Dorian Gray* (1891), London could become a place of secrets, a city in which many people, otherwise normal and sane, could change their form as they moved from street to street, or from drawing room to attic.

Henry James would set his novel of nineteenth-century terrorism in this London. *The Princess Casamassima* (1886) "proceeded quite directly," he wrote, "during the first year of a long residence in London, from the habit of walking the streets. I walked a great deal—for exercise, for amusement, for acquisition, and above all I always walked home at evening's end, when the evening had been spent elsewhere, as happened more often than not."

Dickens, too, told a friend that he had composed *A Christmas Carol* in his head as he walked about "the black streets of London, fifteen and twenty miles, many a night when all the sober folks had gone to bed." The images that came to him then were of spirits and phantoms, aspects of a dream city in which nothing remained stable—least of all the past, the present, or the future, which live like unearthly protagonists in the story Dickens created. The London he made in *A Christmas Carol* is as much haunted by its citizens as inhabited by them.

In the story, Dickens takes Scrooge on a journey in which time and space have no solidity, through a London of the imagination, using fictional registers that would have immense influence on ways in which Christmas is celebrated to this day.

When Scrooge looks out of the window he sees "[t]he air filled with phantoms, wandering hither and thither in restless haste, and moaning as they went." The Ghost who propels Scrooge is merciless and relentless, forcing him, at first, to live in a time when past and present merge. Some of the images he sees are of comfort and joy, but they are experiences in which he cannot share. They are disrupted by what he can hear, as the happy people are discussing him, Scrooge. One man, for example, who is enjoying domestic bliss, says: "I passed his office window; . . . and there he sat alone. Quite alone in the world, I do believe."

Later, Scrooge will see the abode of the Cratchit family. "They were not a handsome family . . . [b]ut they were happy, grateful, pleased with one another, and contented with the time." The family, once they have said grace, consume a goose on Christmas Day. "There never was such a goose. . . . Its tenderness and flavor, size and cheapness, were the themes of universal admiration." Indeed, the Cratchit family themselves, including the doomed Tiny Tim, become the subject of universal admiration. But they too, despite their sweetness, discuss Scrooge, who has to listen as Mrs. Cratchit wishes to drink "the health of such an odious, stingy, hard, unfeeling man as Mr. Scrooge."

Later, in Scrooge's dark night of the soul, he will have also to witness his nephew and the nephew's friends playing a parlor game in which they are asked to guess the identity of "an animal, a live animal, rather a disagreeable animal, a savage animal, an animal that growled and grunted sometimes, and talked sometimes, and lived in London, and walked about the streets." His name, of course, is Scrooge.

Such visions will seem almost innocent compared to the darker ones that are to come as Scrooge will be forced to witness his servants selling his clothes and his curtains as he lies on his deathbed. They will refer to him as "a wicked old screw." Soon, he will be shown the relief and happiness of those in debt to him on hearing of his demise:

"The only emotion, that the Ghost could show him, caused by the event, was one of pleasure."

When his redemption comes, as it must, because what happens to Scrooge in the night has a moral purpose, then the diction of the story itself will lighten, as Scrooge's meanness lightens. The sentence structure and a generosity in rhythm of the prose will reflect the lifting of his burden. "He went to church and walked about the streets, and watched the people hurrying to and fro, and patted children on the head, and questioned beggars, and looked down into the kitchens of houses, and up to the windows; and found that anything could yield him pleasure. He never dreamed that any walk—that anything—could give him so much happiness."

The word *dream* has been transformed, has been taken from its dark, cold, lonely, fearful place, and, instead of being a watchword for frightful imaginings, filled with mockery and unbearable visions, has come to mean an opening of the self, a way of reimagining the world. And so, with that change, from nightmare to sweet reality, from miserliness to giving, from misery to merriness, Christmas came into being. Courtesy of Dickens, we live in its shadow still, and on one cheery, idealized day of the year, as we force Scrooge to appear as merely a distant warning to us all, we become the happy, jolly Cratchits.

Introduction

DECLAN KIELY

Charles Dickens started writing *A Christmas Carol* in mid-October 1843 and finished it just six weeks later, on 2 December. He began the story in the grip of "a hideous cold" that, he told his friend Angela Burdett Coutts, "has taken possession of me to an almost unprecedented extent." To his friend and fellow novelist William Harrison Ainsworth he reported himself "at this moment deaf in the ears, hoarse in the throat, red in the nose, green in the gills, damp in the eyes, twitchy in the joints, and fractious in the temper." But *A Christmas Carol* was a story that Dickens was compelled to write, and he quite literally could not afford to let illness delay him.

To understand what made Dickens so determined to write *A Christmas Carol*—while he was simultaneously preoccupied in writing the next monthly installment of his novel *Martin Chuzzlewit*—we must recall the difficult personal circumstances that beset him, as well as the larger social issues that deeply concerned him, in the fall of 1843.

Dickens shot to fame when *The Pickwick Papers*, published in monthly installments in 1836–37, proved enormously popular with readers. While completing *Pickwick*, he began writing *Oliver Twist*, which was also serialized in monthly parts between 1837 and 1839. He continued without pause for breath and, in 1838, began *Nicholas Nickleby* while he was still writing installments of *Oliver Twist*, finding the creative spark of each new novel in the embers of the preceding work.

Despite his rapid and phenomenal success, Dickens remained uncertain of his economic future as a journalist and novelist. In order to have a fallback option, in December 1839 he enrolled as a law student at the Middle Temple (one of London's four Inns of Court for trainee lawyers), although he never entered the legal profession as a barrister. As if the pace of writing novels for a monthly serialization deadline—and the considerable overlap of *Oliver Twist* and *Nicholas Nickleby*—were not demanding enough, Dickens also inaugurated *Master Humphrey's Clock*, a weekly periodical whose entire contents, despite his original intentions, he was responsible for writing and in which he would publish his next novels, *The Old Curiosity Shop* and *Barnaby Rudge*, between 1840 and 1841.

By the end of 1841, having had his work continuously before the reading public for more than five years, Dickens was concerned about overexposure and exhaustion. Needing to take a break, he arranged with his publisher, Chapman and Hall, to spend the first six months of 1842 touring the United States, on the understanding that he would "keep a note-book" and write about the journey upon his return. Chapman and Hall agreed to a year's paid sabbatical: £150 per month until he started his next novel, rising to £200 per month when the new novel began to appear in print. This was a gamble, for unless this new novel equaled the success of its predecessors, Dickens would effectively be in debt to his publisher to the tune of £1,800.

Chapman and Hall duly published *American Notes for General Circulation* in October 1842, and Dickens began his next novel, *Martin Chuzzlewit*, the following month. Sales figures for this new novel were unexpectedly lower than for his previous publications, however. *The Pickwick Papers* and *Nicholas Nickleby* had sold between 40,000 and 50,000 copies every month, and *The Old Curiosity Shop* had reached 100,000 copies per week at the height of its popularity. In contrast, *Martin Chuzzlewit* was selling only 20,000 copies each month. *American Notes* had also not sold as well as anticipated (although four editions were printed in two months, so it was certainly no failure).

A clause in Dickens's contract allowed the publisher, in the event of poor sales, to deduct £50 from the agreed salary (of £200 per month) for *Martin Chuzzlewit*. As the monthly circulation figures continued to languish at around or under 20,000 copies, William Hall (Edward Chapman's publishing partner) hinted that they might invoke this clause. Dickens flew into a rage, telling John Forster, his close friend and future biographer, that "I am bent on paying Chapman and Hall *down*." He insisted that £50 should immediately be deducted from the £200 he received in monthly payments for *Martin Chuzzlewit*; he also decided, impulsively, that he would break with his publisher altogether, and told Forster that once he had fully repaid his advance, "Mr. Hall shall have a piece of my mind." He made good on both threats.

In December 1839, following the huge success of his first three novels, Dickens—in a state he described as "ecstatic restlessness"—had taken an eleven-year lease on 1 Devonshire Terrace, Regent's Park, the spacious London house that would remain his family's home until 1851. Dickens had the house extensively (and expensively) refurbished before moving in, replacing wooden mantels with marble, trading plain pinewood doors for paneled mahogany, and installing the most modern water closets available. Here he was able to accommodate more comfortably his growing family and entertain his large circle of friends on a lavish scale. In addition to the author's personal groom, the house employed five live-in servants. As Dickens's recent biographer, Michael Slater, notes, "The life-style that by 1840 Dickens had established for himself and his family in Devonshire Terrace certainly required the support of a rising income."

Yet by the fall of 1843, Dickens's income was not rising but falling. His wife was expecting their fifth child (Francis, born in January 1844), and his household expenses were increasing. The lease for 1 Devonshire Terrace had cost £800 and the annual rent was £160. Dickens was painfully aware that he was not earning enough money to sustain his lifestyle and also meet his financial obligations. In a letter to Charles Smithson on 14 November 1843, he ruefully explained: "It was a consequence of the astonishing rapidity of my success and the steady rise of my fame that the enormous profits of these books should flow into other hands than mine."

To make matters even worse, Dickens continued to be tormented by the insolvency of his improvident and impecunious father and younger brothers, whom he referred to bitterly as his "blood-petitioners." In March 1841, *The Times* and other daily London newspapers carried a notice, placed on Dickens's behalf by his solicitors (Thomas Mitton and Charles Smithson), disclaiming any responsibility for debts incurred by anyone bearing the surname "Dickens"—that is, by John Dickens, the author's father. Despite this step, John Dickens continued to solicit loans, on the strength of his son's name and fame, from Dickens's friends and, even more daringly, from his publisher.

Matters came to a head in the fall of 1843, when Dickens was enraged to learn that his father had borrowed money even from Thomas Mitton (with whom Charles Dickens had enjoyed a close friendship since the age of fifteen, when they worked together as clerks in a law firm). He told Mitton on 28 September that

> he [John Dickens] is certain to do it again. There was no help but to pay it, as you so kindly did. But he is sure to do it again. Even now, with the knowledge of him which I have so dearly purchased, I am amazed and confounded by the audacity of his ingratitude. He, and all of them, look upon me as a something to be plucked and torn to pieces for their advantage. They have no idea of, and no care for,

my existence in any other light. My soul sickens at the thought of them.

His father's most recent pleas for money had, he told Mitton, "disgusted me beyond expression." The extent to which Dickens suffered from the continuous financial and emotional strain of his father's clandestine borrowing is made explicit at the close of his letter:

> Nothing makes me so wretched, or so unfit for what I have to do, as these things. They are so entirely beyond my own controul, so far out of my reach, such a drag-chain on my life, that for the time they utterly dispirit me, and weigh me down.

It was in the midst of—and also as a practical response to—this distressing financial crisis that Dickens began composing *A Christmas Carol*. At the beginning of the story, when Ebenezer Scrooge disparages Christmas, he asks his nephew: "What's Christmas Time to you but a time for paying bills without money; a time for finding yourself a year older and not an hour richer; a time for balancing your books and having every item in 'em through a round dozen of months, presented dead against you?" There is more than a touch of sharp personal relevance in this question, given Dickens's predicament as he anticipated the impending Christmastime. It had become imperative for him to write something that would be an immediate commercial success, which is perhaps why, as he "plunged headlong" into its composition, he referred to his new story (in a letter of 24 October) as "a little scheme." Dickens's use of the word "scheme" is a telling indication that he was thinking in terms of a business plan as much as a literary creation.

The character of Scrooge—whose name is an onomatopoeic amalgam of "screw" and "gouge"—is one of Dickens's most vividly grotesque creations. Perhaps Scrooge lives and breathes so authentically on the page because Dickens was able to pour into him, exaggerating and magnifying for stronger effect, some measure of the anger, misanthropy, and obsessive concern for money that oppressed his soul as he began to write the story.

Because Dickens was busily writing for his next publication deadline— the eleventh monthly installment of *Martin Chuzzlewit*—he was initially able to work on *A Christmas Carol* only in the "odd moments of leisure" that were available to him. We get a glimpse of how Dickens was able to create such a powerful story in a matter of only a few weeks in his letter to Forster of 2 November 1843, in which he reported "That I feel my power now, more than I ever did. That I have a greater confidence in myself than I ever had."

Dickens's rate of composition is revealed in a letter by Georgina Hogarth, his sister-in-law, who noted that "an average day's work with him was 2 or 2½ of those sides—or 'slips' as he called them, of M.S. [manuscript]. A very, very hard day's work was 4 of them." That is, he wrote between 1,425 and 2,280 words each day. By the end of November he described "working from morning until night upon my little Christmas Book." Dickens was always able to redirect adverse personal experience into creative energy, transmuting the randomness and sordidness of life into enduring art.

Two days after completing *A Christmas Carol*, on 4 December, Dickens wrote to Mitton "to ask you to turn over in your mind, between this and tomorrow, how I can best put £200 into Coutts's [bank]. For on looking into the matter this morning, for the first time these 6 weeks, I find (to my horror) that I have already overdrawn my account. . . . And therefore I must anticipate the Christmas Book, by the sum I mention, which will enable me to keep comfortable." He added, "I wouldn't trouble you about the money, if it were not a case of necessity. But being so busy, I have let it pass until the very last moment[.]" Dickens expected that by March, when revenues from *A Christmas Carol* would be in hand, he would be moderately rich. This letter, in its original envelope, was subsequently pasted into the front endpapers of the bound manuscript of *A Christmas Carol*, a powerful reminder of the acutely difficult personal circumstances in which Dickens wrote this story.

The question of how he might best be able to put £200 into his bank account, combined with the optimistic prediction that *A Christmas Carol* would make him not only solvent but rich, is depressingly reminiscent of the tone and style of his father's begging letters. It must have made Dickens extremely uncomfortable to write this letter to Mitton, who had already, in July, supplied him with £70 to tide him over until September.

Two weeks after the publication of *A Christmas Carol*, Dickens wrote (in the third person) to his friend Cornelius Felton, professor of Greek at Harvard, about the exhilaration he had felt when writing his story: "Charles Dickens wept, and laughed, and wept again, and excited himself in a most extraordinary manner, in the composition; and thinking whereof, he walked about the black streets of London, fifteen and twenty miles, many a night when all the sober folks had gone to bed."

Dickens wrote to Charles Mackay of the *Morning Chronicle* newspaper, telling him that "I was very much affected by the little Book myself; in various ways, as I wrote it; and had an interest in the idea, which made me reluctant to lay it aside for a moment." The "idea" that Dickens refers to here is his concern with the general condition of the poor, and in particular the suffering of impoverished children. *A Christmas Carol* marks the beginning of a new phase in Dickens's writing, characterized by his more overt use of fiction as an instrument of social change. The composition of the story coincided with a period of intense social activism, and the book can be regarded as a literary extension of his advocacy for social reform, for Dickens had a specific agenda in mind as he wrote it. He would have agreed with Kafka, who said that "a book must be the axe for the frozen sea inside us."

Britain's economic depression of the early 1840s became known to later historians as the "hungry forties." A serious slump in trade in 1839 led to a steep rise in unemployment. Successive bad harvests, exacerbated by the government's control of the price of grain, kept the price of bread artificially high and led to widespread hunger among the poor.

In May 1842, Dickens was appalled to read the revelations in *The Condition and Treatment of the Children Employed in the Mines and Collieries of the United Kingdom*, published following a three-year investigation by a parliamentary commission and compiled by his friend Richard Henry Horne. Dickens promised Macvey Napier, the editor of the Whig quarterly the *Edinburgh Review*, to write an article about the report's findings. In the spring of the following year Dickens described himself as "perfectly stricken down" after reading the Children's Employment Commission's *Second Report*. He contemplated writing and publishing "a very cheap" campaigning pamphlet that would be titled *An Appeal to the People of England on behalf of the Poor Man's Child*. Ultimately, he wrote neither article nor pamphlet, but his indignation continued to smolder.

On 14 September 1843 Dickens visited Samuel Starey's so-called Ragged School in Field Lane, London, which endeavored to provide basic education for severely deprived children living in slums. Following his disturbing visit, Dickens successfully petitioned Angela Burdett Coutts (the wealthiest philanthropist in Britain) to support Starey's efforts. Dickens told her that he had

> very seldom seen, in all the strange and dreadful things I
> have seen in London and elsewhere, anything so shock-
> ing as the dire neglect of soul and body exhibited in these

children. . . . The children in the Jails are almost as common sights to me as my own; but these are worse, for they have not arrived there yet, but are as plainly and certainly travelling there, as they are to their Graves.

The appalling spectacle filled Dickens with dark forebodings about the very future of the nation itself, and he foresaw "that in the prodigious misery and ignorance of the swarming masses of mankind in England, the seeds of its certain ruin are sown."

These Ragged School children are the same "wretched, abject, frightful, hideous, miserable" children with whom the Ghost of Christmas Present confronts Scrooge—the "yellow, meagre, ragged, scowling, wolfish" figures of "Ignorance" and "Want." As social propaganda, *A Christmas Carol* proved to be much more of a "sledge-hammer blow" (a metaphor Dickens was fond of using in relation to his work) than any pamphlet or newspaper article could have been.

Dickens, the consummate craftsman—who described himself creating stories as "the story-weaver at his loom"—was particularly careful in his selection of writing materials and in the fate of his manuscripts. He wrote *A Christmas Carol* in black ink, using his customary goose quill pen, on a mixture of high-quality, unlined papers: "London Superfine" for the title page and preface, and "Bath Superfine" for the narrative. Each sheet measured 8⅞ × 7¼ inches.

As soon as he completed the story on 2 December, he folded the 68-page manuscript vertically and either took or sent it to the printer Bradbury and Evans, which supplanted Chapman and Hall as Dickens's publisher in 1844. As John Butt and Kathleen Tillotson noted in *Dickens at Work* (1957), his printers "had to make do with 'copy' obscure enough to daunt the most experienced compositor. . . . But the compositors were picked men, clean, quick, and accurate." The compositors had to work extremely quickly in order to produce the book in time for the Christmas market. Proofs were evidently sent to Mitton on 4 or 5 December, and Dickens and Forster also proofread the story, but no revised or corrected proofs for *A Christmas Carol* survive.

After the manuscript was returned from the printer, Dickens added this note at the bottom of the title page:

/My own, and only, MS of the Book /
Charles Dickens.

He sent the manuscript to a bookbinder (possibly Thomas Robert Eeles of Cursitor Street, London) to be bound in red morocco—a handsome, durable goatskin leather suitable for dyeing in strong colors such as the rich crimson that was chosen for this binding. It was elegantly decorated in gilt, and the name "Thomas Mitton Esqre" was also stamped in gilt on the front cover. Dickens presented the bound manuscript to his close friend and creditor, possibly as a Christmas gift, and certainly in gratitude for the generous loan of £270 in the preceding six months.

Dickens appears to have made no working notes, outline, plans, or preliminary draft of *A Christmas Carol*. From the mid-1840s on, it had become his custom to draw up quite elaborate summaries and notes prior to beginning each novel in order to adequately track the large number of characters and plot lines he introduced. But given the time pressure to complete *A Christmas Carol* so that copies would be available in time for Christmas, as well as the compelling circumstances of its creation, it should not be surprising that Dickens needed no memoranda to assist him as he worked furiously on the narrative.

The structure of the story is simple. Its five parts—each labeled by Dickens a "stave," or stanza (the verse of a carol or song)—are essentially theatrical in nature. The first and fifth staves function as prologue and epilogue to the story, with the second, third, and fourth staves—which feature the Ghosts of Christmas Past, Present, and Yet to Come— forming the three central acts of a conventional five-act drama.

That Dickens had a dramatic model in mind is evident on the first page of the manuscript, where the ghost of Hamlet's father is introduced, leading to a digression concerning the character of Hamlet that Dickens seems to have immediately recognized as superfluous and potentially distracting from the scenario he was establishing. Dickens was clearly seeking, in the first section of his story, to achieve the same level of thrilling dramatic intensity with the entrance of Marley's ghost as Shakespeare achieved in the first scene of *Hamlet*, in which Horatio and the sentinels of the watch are harrowed "with fear and wonder."

A good example of Dickens's creative economy, and an important factor that also helped him complete *A Christmas Carol* in only six weeks, was his inspired choice of plot and protagonist, for which he drew heavily on a minor character from one of the digressive short stories in *The Pickwick Papers*. In that novel, Mr. Wardle narrates the story of Gabriel Grubb, an old misanthropic sexton (church bell ringer and gravedigger). Grubb, who is "an ill-conditioned cross-grained surly fellow . . . who consorted with nobody but himself," is recognizably a prototype of Ebenezer Scrooge.

Refusing to participate in the celebration of Christmas and instead digging graves on Christmas Eve, Grubb is captured by goblins and tortured by being shown poignant scenes of poverty and human suffering, a painful experience that ultimately leads to his reformation. With *A Christmas Carol*, then, Dickens elaborated a plot and character from his earlier fiction to meet his most immediate needs.

There may also be an even earlier archetype of Ebenezer Scrooge on which Dickens drew. Professor Michael Hancher has argued persuasively for Dickens's authorship of a fictional letter to the editor of the *Athenaeum* (published on 7 January 1832) that, in theme and tone, strongly foreshadows the character of Scrooge. That letter, titled "'Merry Christmas to You;' or, Wishes Not Horses" and signed "Your constant Reader, and / Occasional Writer, / C. D.," delivers a firmly tongue-in-cheek Swiftian diatribe against the use of the epithet "merry." C. D. concludes his letter by posing this dyspeptic question: "What wonder, then, if I hate the sound of that which is to me *but* a sound?—if I begin to doubt whether there is, in reality, any such thing as a merry Christmas."[*]

Although the bold lineaments of structure, plot, and protagonist were all firmly in Dickens's mind at the outset, the manuscript reveals that in the process of writing the story he changed his mind innumerable times about small but significant details. For instance, Bob Cratchit's sickly son is first introduced to the reader on page 37 as "Tiny Fred," a name that Dickens seems to have changed at once to the more memorably alliterative "Tiny Tim." It is clear from the interlinear revisions in the manuscript that Bob Cratchit, too, came by his name only gradually.

Lower down on the same page, an exchange between Scrooge and the Ghost of Christmas Present concerning Tiny Tim's health and future prospects is deleted with eight diagonal pen strokes, effectively putting the text in a still-legible box. Dickens thereby indicated to himself that this portion was not to be permanently struck out but only moved to improve the flow of his narrative. It is an example of just how acutely aware Dickens was, as he wrote, of the greater dramatic effect that could be achieved by withholding information until later in the

---

[*] See Michael Hancher, "Dickens's First Effusion," *Dickens Quarterly* 31 (2014): 285–97; the article includes the full text of the letter (pp. 287–90), which is strikingly coincident with several passages in *A Christmas Carol*.

scene (page 39 of the manuscript), allowing his readers to develop feel-
ings of sympathy for Tiny Tim, as he is depicted as an adored altruistic
presence in the Cratchit family home, before the ghost's devastating
prediction: "The child will die."

Oddly, the manuscript is silent about Tiny Tim's ultimate fate. Perhaps in his rush to conclude the story, Dickens neglected to explicitly
inform readers in the last pages of the manuscript whether Tiny Tim
lived or died. This omission was probably spotted by Mitton or Forster, and Dickens must have added this sentence, a decidedly hurried
construction, to the proofs: "and to Tiny Tim, who did NOT die, he
[Scrooge] was a second father." It is also possible, since Tiny Tim's
benediction comprises the final words of the manuscript, that Dickens originally trusted his readers to infer that the child survived and
flourished.

Dickens's heavily corrected manuscript reveals additional insights into
his working methods, giving readers a greater appreciation of his art-
istry. The hundreds of revisions vividly convey the sense of an author
writing at a fast pace, usually experiencing his second thoughts and
changes of mind in the heat of original composition, striking out words
and phrases and replacing them with a seemingly unhesitating, continuous flow of new words on the same line.

For example, at the end of Stave IV (page 60 of the manuscript),
the last seven words of the final paragraph, following "dwindled down

into a bedpost," are deleted. The struck-out words read: "which he knew to be his own." Dickens seems to have realized that this information undermined the suspenseful, cliff-hanger ending he sought to achieve at the end of dramatic scenes, and the encounter with the inscrutable hooded phantom, the Ghost of Christmas Yet to Come, is arguably the most dramatic in the entire story. To tell readers that the bedpost was Scrooge's own would have given too much away; ending the episode in this way would have been too comforting (for Scrooge and the reader). So Dickens changed his mind, struck out the words, and inserted the spiral swirl (or "flourish") that appears at the end of each stave in the manuscript: the cue to the printer that the chapter had ended. Then Dickens reached for a new sheet of blank paper and began the next and final stave with life-affirming alacrity: "Yes! And the bedpost was his own."

There is invariably a rapid, bold confidence about Dickens's pen strokes, and this is especially evident in the manuscript of *A Christmas Carol*. He deleted text with a cursive and continuous looping movement of the pen—rendering his first thoughts exasperatingly difficult to determine—and replaced canceled words with fewer words or with more active verbs to achieve greater concision, vividness, and immediacy.

A good example of this practice may be seen at the beginning of Stave III (page 31 of the manuscript), where Dickens deleted almost the entire first line and replaced the preamble with the single present-tense verb "Awaking," which thrusts the action forward. There is evidence that Dickens occasionally paused for thought as he wrote *A Christmas*

Carol, but little evidence that these pauses extended longer than a few moments. The numerous interlineal revisions, most often squeezed onto the page in smaller than usual handwriting, suggest that he habitually revisited the text—possibly at the end of a writing session, or when the entire story had been completed—to rewrite and improve. The overwhelming impression conveyed by the physical appearance of the manuscript is that it was a production into which Dickens concentrated all of his prodigious energy. As the collector Robert H. Taylor observed, "Every page of it is scored all through with corrections, yet its gusto and exuberance are as fresh as though it had been set down without alteration."

Dickens also focused a great deal of attention on the publication of the book, which marked the first time any of his writing had been issued in a single volume. In order to maximize the profit on his latest work, he arranged with Chapman and Hall to publish the book on commission: that is, he would be personally responsible for all of the production costs, but instead of receiving only a royalty, he would net the income from sales. He anticipated that *A Christmas Carol* would make him £1,000.

In his eagerness to make the book as physically attractive as possible while remaining reasonably affordable (at five shillings a copy), Dickens commissioned John Leech to create eight original illustrations, four of which were full-page hand-colored etchings (a colorful—and expensive—bibliographic feature that Dickens was never to repeat). He selected salmon-brown cloth for the binding, a gilt design for the cover and spine, gilt edges, a half-title page printed in blue, and a title page printed in two colors. Dickens further ran up production costs by objecting to the title page originally printed in green and red, opting for blue and red instead.

By the time copies appeared in bookshops on 19 December, every improvement and enhancement of the book's physical appearance had narrowed Dickens's profit margin. Sixty percent of the cost of the book went to the binding and color illustrations, and an additional 16 percent to printing the text and the four other engraved illustrations. Advertising and incidentals entailed further expenses.

Following a series of laudatory reviews, by Christmas Eve every one of the 6,000 copies of the first print run had completely sold out. It was, as Dickens proclaimed, "a most prodigious success—the greatest, I think, I have ever achieved." On 2 January 1844, Dickens reported excitedly to Mitton: "The subscription in the City (exclusive of the West End) for the Second Edition of the Carol, was 1500. They have consequently printed 3000 additional, instead of 2, making in all 9000, and not 8. Hurrah, say I!"

But Dickens's ebullience was to be short-lived. Although the book continued to sell well, with a third edition advertised on 20 January, on the morning of 11 February Dickens wrote to Forster in a dreadful panic:

> Such a night as I have passed! I really believed I should never get up again, until I had passed through all the horrors of a fever. I found the Carol accounts awaiting me, and they were the cause of it. The first six thousand copies show a profit of £230! And the last four will yield as much

more. I had set my heart and soul upon a Thousand
[pounds], clear. What a wonderful thing it is, that such a
great success should occasion me such intolerable anxiety
and disappointment! My year's bills, unpaid, are so terrific,
that all the energy and determination I can possibly exert
will be required to clear me before I go abroad; which, if
next June come and find me alive, I shall do.

In fact, Dickens received only £137 from Chapman and Hall the
next day, and another £49 on 14 February. Even by the end of 1844
he had received only £726, considerably less than the £1,000 he had
expected. He told Mitton that he was "not only on my beam ends,
but tilted over on the other side. Nothing so unexpected and utterly
disappointing, has ever befallen me. That you know. The bill for £200
must be provided for. To that, I mean to devote this precious balance.
The rest must be worked round somehow. . . . Nothing upholds me
under this, but the very circumstance that makes it so tremendous—the
wonderful success of the book."

The book was also proving to be a successful enterprise for Purley's
Illustrated Library, a publisher that had taken the liberty of producing a pirated edition of A Christmas Carol. Through Mitton, Dickens
initiated a successful action to sue for copyright infringement, but
the publisher subsequently declared bankruptcy. To further add to his
financial woes, Dickens was obliged to pay the £700 in legal costs that
the action incurred.

Despite all these troubles, the critical and longer-term financial success of *A Christmas Carol* initiated the lucrative series of Christmas books that Dickens published over the next several years: *The Chimes* (1844), *The Cricket on the Hearth* (1845), *The Battle of Life* (1846), and *The Haunted Man* (1848). Each of these was written largely in response to the public demand for a Christmas book unleashed by the success of *A Christmas Carol.*

In 1875, five years after Dickens's death, Thomas Mitton sold the manuscript of *A Christmas Carol* to Francis Harvey, a London bookseller. Harvey is believed to have paid Mitton £50 for it, and he sold it almost immediately to Henry George Churchill, a private collector who (according to the Dickens scholar F. G. Kitton), when he heard that the manuscript was for sale, "immediately hailed a cab to convey him to the West End where he ascertained the price, wrote out a cheque for the amount, and bore off the prize in triumph."

Churchill retained the manuscript in his collection until 1882, but then decided to sell it through a bookseller named Bennett, who was based in Birmingham, England. Crowds reportedly gathered there for an opportunity to view the manuscript before it was sold for £200 to the London booksellers Robson and Kerslake. It was soon sold again, this time for £300, to Stuart M. Samuel, who bought it purely as an investment.

Sometime before 1900, the famous American financier Pierpont

Morgan acquired the manuscript from the London bookseller J. Pearson & Co., which had acquired it in 1890 from Stuart M. Samuel for £1,000. Having more than tripled its price in less than a decade, the manuscript had certainly proved its value as an investment. The amount Morgan paid for *A Christmas Carol* remains unknown, but it would most likely have cost him 10 or 20 percent more than what Pearson had paid Samuel.

On Morgan's death in 1913 the manuscript was bequeathed to J. P. Morgan Jr., who in 1924 established the Pierpont Morgan Library in his father's honor. The manuscript became accessible to both scholars and visitors to the library. *A Christmas Carol* remains one of the most important British literary manuscripts in the Morgan's collection and a perennial favorite with visitors; it is displayed every year throughout December. This facsimile edition enables readers to enjoy the manuscript all the year round.

In preparation for the creation of a facsimile, the manuscript received extensive treatment by conservators at the Morgan's Thaw Conservation Center. First it was disbound, a painstaking process to remove the pages from their original binding. Then, once removed, each sheet was submerged in a shallow bath of water and alcohol. Doing so dissolved the adhesive that had been used, probably sometime between 1910 and 1920, to attach barely visible, fine silk gauze to the blank sides of each sheet of the manuscript. This silk gauze was carefully lifted away from the paper.

"Silking" was once a popular technique for strengthening or reinforcing paper, but it has fallen out of favor and use. Over time, the silk tends to become brittle and ineffective, and can cause paper to darken and discolor. Once de-silked, each sheet was submerged in a shallow bath of calcium carbonate–enriched deionized water and alcohol, then lightly brushed to remove any residual adhesive. A second bath completed the washing process.

Washing in deionized water enriched with calcium carbonate neutralizes soluble acids. This step is essential because Dickens, like most writers of his time, used black iron-gall ink that, to the advantage of later generations of readers, was water-resistant and adhered permanently to the surface of the paper. It is highly acidic, however, and after many years it can cause some paper to deteriorate drastically. The rich black tone of this ink is also usually lost over time, turning a dark brown, as can be seen in Dickens's manuscript.

After washing, each sheet of the manuscript was air-dried, and the drying process was completed by placing the sheets between blotters under weight for several days. When completely dry, the sheets were examined closely, and any small tears or weakened parts were mended using thin Japanese tissue and diluted wheat-starch paste. Happily, the conservators determined that Dickens's manuscript of *A Christmas Carol* was in remarkably good condition, with little evidence of corrosion from the ink or degradation from the silking (thanks, in large part, to the high-quality paper that Dickens had used).

All the newly restored pages—now considerably closer in color, texture, and overall appearance to the manuscript that Dickens had bound for Thomas Mitton in December 1843—were digitally photographed in full color for the first time. Every nuance of Dickens's handwriting, described by the biographer Peter Ackroyd as "distinctive, clear but nervous," is captured in these high-resolution photofacsimile pages.

Forty years after the first publication of *A Christmas Carol*, on 5 March 1883, Vincent van Gogh wrote to his friend and fellow painter Anthon van Rappard: "This week I bought a new 6-penny edition of *Christmas carol* and *Haunted man* by Dickens. . . . I find *all* of Dickens beautiful, but those two tales—I've re-read them almost every year since I was a boy, and they always seem new to me."

Readers who share van Gogh's admiration for *A Christmas Carol* will discover, through this facsimile edition of Dickens's original manuscript, a new and deeper appreciation for this "Ghostly little book" and its enduring afterlife.

Declan Kiely
Robert H. Taylor Curator and Department Head
Literary and Historical Manuscripts
The Morgan Library & Museum

A Note on the Transcription

The text facing the manuscript facsimile represents the most faithful transcription to date. No attempt has been made to transcribe the words or phrases that Dickens deleted; his method of striking out rejected text renders his original thought, in most circumstances, all but illegible. The handwritten manuscript, used by the printers to set type for the first edition in 1843, differs only slightly in narrative (see the footnote on page 133). Some of the peculiarities of Dickens's spelling have been silently corrected. Dickens's "rhetorical" style of punctuation, based on speech rhythms rather than strict grammatical sense, involved frequent use of colons, semi-colons, and dashes. These have been retained as they appear in the manuscript and first edition.

[Title]

A Christmas Carol
    In Prose;
Being a Short Story of Christmas.
    By Charles Dickens

The Illustrations by John Leech

Chapman and Hall 186 Strand
MDCCC XL III.

[My own, and only MS of the Book]
Charles Dickens

/Title/

A Christmas Carol

IN PROSE:

Being a Ghost Story of Christmas.

By Charles Dickens

THE ILLUSTRATIONS BY JOHN LEECH

CHAPMAN & HALL 186 STRAND
MDCCCXL III.

/My own, and only, MS of the Book/
Charles Dickens

Preface.

I have endeavoured in this Ghostly little book, to raise the Ghost of an Idea', which shall not put my readers out of humour with themselves, with each other, with the season, or with me. May it haunt their houses pleasantly, and no one wish to lay it!

Their faithful friend and Servant
CD.

December 1843.

PREFACE

I have endeavoured, in this Ghostly little book, to raise the Ghost of an Idea, which shall not put my readers out of humour with themselves, with each other, with the season, or with me. May it haunt their houses pleasantly, and no one wish to lay it!

Their faithful friend and Servant,
CD.

December 1843.

Stave I.

Marley's Ghost.

Marley was dead: to begin with. There is no doubt whatever, about that. The register of his burial was signed by the clergyman, the clerk, the undertaker, and the chief mourner. Scrooge signed it; and Scrooge's name was good upon 'change, for anything he put his hand to. Old Marley was as dead as a door-nail.

Mind! I don't mean to say that I know, of my own knowledge, what there is particularly dead about a door-nail. I might have been inclined, myself, to regard a coffin-nail as the deadest piece of ironmongery in the trade. But the wisdom of our ancestors is in the simile; and my unhallowed hands shall not disturb it, or the country's done for. You will therefore permit me to repeat, emphatically, that Marley was as dead as a door-nail.

Scrooge knew he was dead? Of course he did. How could it be otherwise? Scrooge and he were partners for I don't know how many years. Scrooge was his sole executor, his sole administrator, his sole assign, his sole residuary legatee, his sole friend and sole mourner. And even Scrooge was not so dreadfully cut up by the sad event, but that he was an excellent man of business on the very day of the funeral, and solemnised it with an undoubted bargain.

The mention of Marley's funeral brings me back to the point I started from. There is no doubt that Marley was dead. This must be distinctly understood, or nothing wonderful can come of the story I am going to relate. If we were not perfectly convinced that Hamlet's Father died before the play began, there would be nothing more remarkable in his taking a stroll at night, in an easterly wind, upon his own ramparts, than there would be in any other middle-aged gentleman rashly turning out after dark in a breezy spot — say Saint Paul's churchyard for instance — literally to astonish his son's weak mind.

Scrooge never painted out old Marley's name. There it

STAVE I.

Marley's Ghost.

Marley was dead: to begin with. There is no doubt whatever, about that. The register of his burial was signed by the clergyman, the clerk, the undertaker, and the chief mourner. Scrooge signed it; and Scrooge's name was good upon 'change, for anything he chose to put his hand to. Old Marley was as dead as a door-nail.

Mind! I don't mean to say that I know, of my own knowledge, what there is particularly dead about a door-nail. I might have been inclined, myself, to regard a coffin-nail as the deadest piece of Ironmongery in the trade. But the wisdom of our ancestors is in the simile; and my unhallowed hands shall not disturb it, or the country's done for. You will therefore permit me to repeat, emphatically, that Marley was as dead as a door-nail.

Scrooge knew he was dead. Of course he did. How could it be otherwise? Scrooge and he were partners for I don't know how many years. Scrooge was his sole executor, his sole administrator, his sole assign, his sole residuary legatee: his sole friend and sole mourner. And even Scrooge was not so dreadfully cut up by the sad event, but that he was an excellent man of business on the very day of the funeral, and solemnised it with an undoubted bargain.

The mention of Marley's Funeral brings me back to the point I started from. There is no doubt that Marley was dead. This must be distinctly understood, or nothing wonderful can come of the story I am going to relate. If we were not perfectly convinced that Hamlet's Father died before the play began, there would be nothing more remarkable in his taking a stroll at night, in an Easterly wind, upon his own ramparts, than there would be in any other middle-aged gentleman rashly turning out after dark, in a breezy spot—say Saint Paul's Churchyard for instance—literally to astonish his son's weak mind.

Scrooge never painted out Old Marley's name. There it

stood, years afterwards, above the warehouse door: Scrooge and Marley. The firm was known as Scrooge and Marley. Sometimes people new to the business called Scrooge Scrooge; and sometimes Marley, but he answered to both names: it was all the same to him.

Oh! But he was a tight-fisted hand at the grind-stone, Scrooge! a squeezing, wrenching, grasping, scraping, clutching, covetous old sinner! Hard and sharp as flint, from which no steel had ever struck out generous fire; secret, and self-contained, and solitary as an oyster. The cold within him ____ his old features, nipped his pointed nose, shrivelled his cheek, stiffened his gait; made his eyes red, his thin lips blue; and spoke out shrewdly in his grating voice. A frosty rime was on his head, and on his eyebrows, and his wiry chin. He carried his own low temperature always about with him; he iced his office in the dog-days; and didn't thaw it one degree at Christmas.

External heat and cold had little influence on Scrooge. No warmth could warm, no wintry weather chill him. No wind that blew was bitterer than he, no falling snow was more intent upon its purpose, no pelting rain less open to entreaty. Foul weather didn't know where to have him. The heaviest rain, and snow, and hail, and sleet could boast of the advantage over him in only one respect. They often "came down" handsomely, and Scrooge never did.

Nobody ever stopped him in the street to say, with gladsome looks, "My dear Scrooge, how are you? when will you come to see me?" No beggars implored him to bestow a trifle, no children asked him what it was o'clock, no man or woman ever once in all his life enquired the way to such and such a place, of Scrooge. Even the blind men's dogs appeared to know him, and when they saw him coming on, would tug their owners into door-ways and up courts: and then would wag their tails as though they said, "no eye at all is better than an evil eye, dark master!"

But what did Scrooge care? It was the very thing he liked. To edge his way along the crowded paths of life, warning all human sympathy to keep its distance, was what the knowing ones call "nuts" to Scrooge.

Once upon a time — of all the good days in the year, on Christmas Eve — old Scrooge sat busy in his counting-house. It was cold, bleak, biting weather: foggy withal: and he could hear the

stood, years afterwards, above the warehouse door—Scrooge and Marley. The firm
was known as Scrooge and Marley. Sometimes people new to the business called
Scrooge Scrooge, and sometimes Marley, but he answered to both names: it was
all the same to him.

Oh! But he was a tight-fisted hand at the grindstone, Scrooge! A squeezing,
wrenching, grasping, scraping, clutching, covetous old sinner! Hard and sharp as
flint, from which no steel had ever struck out generous fire; secret, and self-
contained and solitary as an oyster. The cold within him froze his old features,
nipped his pointed nose, shrivelled his cheek, stiffened his gait; made his eyes red,
his thin lips blue; and spoke out shrewdly in his grating voice. A frosty rime was
on his head, and on his eyebrows, and his wiry chin. He carried his own low
temperature always about him; he iced his office in the dog-days; and didn't thaw
it one degree at Christmas.

External heat and cold had little influence on Scrooge. No warmth could
warm, nor wintry weather chill him. No wind that blew was bitterer than he, no
falling snow was more intent upon its purpose, no pelting rain less open to
entreaty. Foul weather didn't know where to have him. The heaviest rain, and
snow, and hail, and sleet could boast of the advantage over him in only one
respect. They often "came down" handsomely: and Scrooge never did.

Nobody ever stopped him in the street to say, with gladsome looks, "My dear
Scrooge how are you? when will you come to see me?" No beggars implored him
to bestow a trifle, no children asked him what it was o'clock, no man or woman
ever once in all his life inquired the way to such and such a place, of Scrooge.
Even the blindmen's dogs appeared to know him, and when they saw him coming
on, would tug their owners into doorways and up courts: and then would wag
their tails as though they said, "no eye at all, is better than an evil eye, dark
master!"

But what did Scrooge care? It was the very thing he liked. To edge his way
along the crowded paths of life, warning all human sympathy to keep its distance,
was what the knowing ones call "nuts" to Scrooge.

Once upon a time—of all the good days in the year, on Christmas Eve—old
Scrooge sat busy in his counting house. It was cold, bleak, biting weather: foggy
withal: and he could hear the

people in the court ~~outside~~ go ~~cheerily~~ up and down, beating their hands upon their breasts, and stamping their feet upon the pavement. stones to warm them. The City clocks had only just gone three, but it was quite dark already - it had not been light, all day - and candles were flaring in the windows of the neighbouring offices, like ruddy smears upon the palpable brown air. The ~~streets~~ fog came pouring in at every chink and keyhole, and was so dense without, that ~~although the court was of the narrowest~~ the houses opposite were mere phantoms. To see the dingy cloud come ~~drooping down~~ obscuring everything, one might have thought that nature lived hard by, and was brewing on a large scale. The door of Scrooge's counting-house was open that he might keep his eye upon ~~the~~ his clerk, who in a dismal little cell beyond - a sort of tank - was copying letters. Scrooge had a very small fire, but the clerk's fire was so ~~very~~ much smaller that it looked like one coal. But he couldn't replenish it, for Scrooge kept the coal-box in his own room; and ~~the clerk~~ ~~the master~~ ~~came in with the shovel~~ ~~the~~ ~~meaning for them to part~~ the clerk put on his white comforter, ~~and tried to warm himself at the candle; in which, not being a man of a strong imagination, he failed.~~

"A merry christmas, uncle! God save you!" cried a cheerful voice. It was the voice of Scrooge's nephew ~~Fred~~ who came upon him so quickly that this was the first intimation he had of his approach.

"Bah!" said Scrooge, "Humbug!"

He had ~~walked~~ so ~~fast~~ in the fog and frost, this nephew of Scrooge's, that he was all in a glow; his face was ruddy and handsome; his eyes sparkled and his breath smoked again.

"Christmas a humbug, uncle!" said Scrooge's nephew. "You don't mean that, I'm sure."

"I do," said Scrooge. "Merry christmas! What right have you to be merry? what reason have you to be merry? You're poor enough."

"Come then," returned the nephew gaily. "What right have you to be dismal? what reason have you to be morose? You're rich enough."

Scrooge having no better answer ready read on the spur of the moment, said Bah! again - and followed it up with Humbug.

"Don't be cross, uncle," said the nephew.

"What else can I be," returned the uncle, "when I live in such

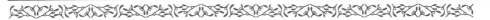

people in the court outside, go wheezing up and down, beating their hands upon their breasts, and stamping their feet upon the pavement-stones to warm them. The city clocks had only just gone three, but it was quite dark already—it had not been light all day—and candles were flaring in the windows of the neighbouring offices, like ruddy smears upon the palpable brown air. The fog came pouring in at every chink and keyhole, and was so dense without, that although the court was of the narrowest the houses opposite were mere phantoms. To see the dingy cloud come drooping down, obscuring everything, one might have thought that Nature lived hard by, and was brewing on a large scale.

The door of Scrooge's counting house was open that he might keep his eye upon his clerk, who in a dismal little cell beyond—a sort of tank—was copying letters. Scrooge had a very small fire, but the clerk's fire was so very much smaller that it looked like one coal. But he couldn't replenish it, for Scrooge kept the coal box in his own room; and so surely as the clerk came in with the shovel, the master predicted that it would be necessary for them to part. Wherefore the clerk put on his white comforter, and tried to warm himself at the candle; in which effort, not being a man of a strong imagination, he failed.

"A merry Christmas, uncle! God save you!" cried a cheerful voice. It was the voice of Scrooge's nephew, who came upon him so quickly that this was the first intimation he had of his approach.

"Bah!" said Scrooge, "Humbug."

He had so heated himself with rapid walking in the fog and frost, this nephew of Scrooge's, that he was all in a glow; his face was ruddy and handsome; his eyes sparkled; and his breath smoked again.

"Christmas a humbug, uncle!" said Scrooge's nephew. "You don't mean that, I am sure."

"I do," said Scrooge. "Merry Christmas! what right have you to be merry? what reason have you to be merry? You're poor enough."

"Come then," returned the nephew gaily. "What right have you to be dismal? what reason have you to be morose? You're rich enough."

Scrooge having no better answer ready on the spur of the moment, said, Bah! again—and followed it up with Humbug.

"Don't be cross, uncle," said the nephew.

"What else can I be?" returned the uncle, "when I live in such

4

a world of fools as this? Merry christmas! out upon merry christmas! what's christmas time to you but a time for paying bills without money; a time for finding yourself a year older and not an hour richer; a time for balancing your books and having every item in 'em through a round dozen of months presented dead against you. If I could work my will," said Scrooge indignantly, "every idiot who goes about with 'merry christmas' on his lips, should be boiled with his own pudding, and buried with a stake of holly through his heart. He should!"

"Uncle!" pleaded the nephew.

"Nephew!" returned the uncle, sternly, "keep christmas in your own way, and let me keep it in mine."

"Keep it!" said Scrooge's nephew. "But you don't keep it."

"Let me leave it alone then," said Scrooge. "Much good may it do you! Much good it has ever done you!"

"There are many things from which I might have derived good, by which I have not profited, I dare say," returned the nephew. "christmas among the rest. But I am sure I have always thought of christmas time, when it has come round — as a good time: a kind, forgiving, charitable, pleasant time: the only time I know of, in the long calendar of the year, when men and women seem by one consent to open their shut-up hearts, freely, and to think of people below them as if they really were fellow-passengers to the grave, and not another race of creatures bound on other journeys. And therefore, uncle, though it has never put a scrap of gold or silver in my pocket, I believe that it has done me good, and will do me good; and I say God bless it!"

The clerk in the tank involuntarily applauded. Becoming immediately sensible of the impropriety, he poked the fire, and extinguished the last frail spark for ever.

"Let me hear another sound from you!" said Scrooge, "and you'll keep your christmas by losing your situation. You're quite a powerful speaker," he added, turning to his nephew. "I wonder you don't go into Parliament."

"Don't be angry, uncle. Come! Dine with us tomorrow."

Scrooge said that he would see him — yes, indeed he did. He went the whole length of the expression, and said that he would see him in that extremity first.

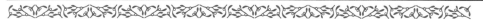

a world of fools as this? Merry Christmas! Out upon merry Christmas! What's Christmas Time to you but a time for paying bills without money; a time for finding yourself a year older and not an hour richer; a time for balancing your books and having every item in 'em through a round dozen of months, presented dead against you? If I could work my will," said Scrooge, indignantly, "every idiot who goes about with 'Merry Christmas' on his lips, should be boiled with his own pudding, and buried with a stake of holly through his heart. He should!"

"Uncle!" pleaded the nephew.

"Nephew!" returned the uncle, sternly, "keep Christmas in your own way, and let me keep it in mine."

"Keep it!" repeated Scrooge's nephew. "But you don't keep it."

"Let me leave it alone then," said Scrooge. "Much good may it do you! Much good it has ever done you!"

"There are many things from which I might have derived good, by which I have not profited, I dare say," returned the nephew. "Christmas among the rest. But I am sure I have always thought of Christmas Time, when it has come round—apart from the veneration due to its sacred name and origin, if anything belonging to it can be apart from that—as a good time: a kind, forgiving, charitable, pleasant time: the only time I know of, in the long calendar of the year, when men and women seem by one consent to open their shut-up hearts, freely, and to think of people below them as if they really were fellow-passengers to the grave, and not another race of creatures bound on other journeys. And therefore, uncle, though it has never put a scrap of gold or silver in my pocket, I believe that it *has* done me good, and *will* do me good; and I say God bless it!"

The clerk in the tank involuntarily applauded. Becoming immediately sensible of the impropriety, he poked the fire, and extinguished the last frail spark for ever.

"Let me hear another sound from *you*," said Scrooge, "and you'll keep your Christmas by losing your situation. You're quite a powerful speaker," he added, turning to his nephew. "I wonder you don't go into Parliament."

"Don't be angry, uncle. Come! Dine with us tomorrow."

Scrooge said that he would see him—yes, indeed he did. He went the whole length of the expression, and said that he would see him in that extremity first.

5

"But why?" cried Scrooge's nephew. "Why?"

"Why did you get married?" said Scrooge.

"Because I fell in love."

"Because you fell in love!" growled Scrooge, as if that were the only one thing in the world more ridiculous than a merry christmas. "Good afternoon!"

"Nay, uncle, but you never came to see me before that happened. Why give it as a reason for not coming now?"

"Good afternoon," said Scrooge. "I ask nothing of you."

"I want nothing from you; why cannot we be friends?"

"Good afternoon," said Scrooge.

"I am sorry, with all my heart, to find you so resolute. We have never had any quarrel, to which I have been a party. But I have made the trial in homage to christmas, and I'll keep my christmas humour to the last. So a merry christmas, uncle!"

"Good afternoon!" said Scrooge.

"and a happy new Year!"

"Good afternoon!" said Scrooge.

His nephew left the room without an angry word, notwithstanding. He stopped at the outer door to bestow the greetings of the season on the clerk, who, cold as he was, was warmer than Scrooge: for he returned them cordially.

"There's another fellow," muttered Scrooge, who overheard him: "my clerk, with fifteen shillings a week, and a wife and family, talking about a merry christmas. I'll retire to Bedlam."

This lunatic, in letting Scrooge's nephew out, had let two other people in. They were portly gentlemen, pleasant to behold, and now stood, with their hats off, in Scrooge's office. They had books and papers in their hands, and bowed to him.

"Scrooge and Marley's, I believe," said one of the gentlemen, referring to his list. "Have I the pleasure of addressing Mr Scrooge, or Mr Marley?" "Mr Marley has been dead these seven years," Scrooge replied. "He died seven years ago, this very night."

"We have no doubt his liberality is well represented by his surviving partner," said the gentleman, presenting his credentials.

It certainly was, for they had been two kindred spirits. At the ominous word liberality, Scrooge frowned, and shook his head, and handed the credentials back.

"But why," cried Scrooge's nephew. "Why?"

"Why did you get married?" said Scrooge.

"Because I fell in love."

"Because you fell in love!" growled Scrooge, as if that were the only one thing in the world more ridiculous than a merry Christmas. "Good afternoon!"

"Nay, uncle, but you never came to see me before that happened. Why give it as a reason for not coming now?"

"Good afternoon," said Scrooge.

"I want nothing from you; I ask nothing of you; why cannot we be friends?"

"Good afternoon," said Scrooge.

"I am sorry, with all my heart, to find you so resolute. We have never had any quarrel to which I have been a party. But I have made the trial in homage to Christmas, and I'll keep my Christmas humour to the last. So a merry Christmas, uncle!"

"Good afternoon!" said Scrooge.

"And a happy new year!"

"Good afternoon!" said Scrooge.

His nephew left the room without an angry word, notwithstanding. He stopped at the outer door to bestow the greetings of the season on the clerk, who, cold as he was, was warmer than Scrooge: for he returned them cordially.

"There's another fellow," muttered Scrooge; who overheard him, "my clerk, with fifteen shillings a week, and a wife and family, talking about a merry Christmas. I'll retire to Bedlam."

This lunatic, in letting Scrooge's nephew out, had let two other people in. They were portly gentlemen, pleasant to behold, and now stood, with their hats off, in Scrooge's office. They had books and papers in their hands, and bowed to him.

"Scrooge and Marley's, I believe," said one of the gentlemen, referring to his list. "Have I the pleasure of addressing Mr. Scrooge, or Mr. Marley?"

"Mr. Marley has been dead these seven years," Scrooge replied. "He died seven years ago, this very night."

"We have no doubt his liberality is well represented by his surviving partner," said the gentleman, presenting his credentials.

It certainly was, for they had been two kindred spirits. At the ominous word liberality, Scrooge frowned, and shook his head, and handed the credentials back.

"at this festive season of the year, Mr Scrooge," said the gentleman, taking up a pen, "it is more than usually desirable that we should make some slight provision for the poor and destitute, who suffer greatly at the present time. Many thousands are in want of common necessaries; hundreds of thousands are in want of common comforts Sir."

"are there no prisons?" asked Scrooge.

"Plenty of prisons," said the gentleman, laying down the pen again.

"and the union workhouses? demanded Scrooge. "are they still in operation?"

"They are. Still," returned the gentleman, "I wish I could say they were not."

"The Treadmill and the Poor Law are in full vigour then?" said Scrooge.

"Both very busy Sir."

"Oh! I was afraid from what you said at first that something had occurred to stop them in their useful course," said Scrooge. "I'm very glad to hear it."

"Under the impression that they scarcely furnish Christian cheer of mind or body to the multitude," returned the gentleman, "a few of us are endeavouring to raise a fund to buy the poor some meat and drink and means of warmth. We choose this time because it is a time of all others when want is keenly felt and abundance rejoices. What shall I put you down for?"

"Nothing," Scrooge replied.

"You wish to be anonymous?"

"I wish to be left alone," said Scrooge. "Since you ask me what I wish, gentlemen, that is my answer. I don't make merry myself at Christmas, and I can't afford to make idle people merry. I help to support the establishments I have mentioned—they cost enough; and those who are badly off must go there."

"Many can't go there; and many would rather die."

"If they would rather die," said Scrooge, "they had better do it, and decrease the surplus population. Besides; excuse me. I don't know that."

"But you might know it," observed the gentleman.

"It's not my business," Scrooge returned. "It's enough for a man to understand his own business, and not to interfere with other peoples. Mine occupies me constantly. Good afternoon gentlemen!"

Seeing clearly that it was useless to pursue their point, the gentlemen withdrew; and Scrooge resumed his labours with an improved opinion of himself, and in a more facetious temper than was usual with him.

"At this festive season of the year, Mr. Scrooge," said the gentleman, taking up a pen, "it is more than usually desirable that we should make some slight provision for the poor and destitute, who suffer greatly at the present time. Many thousands are in want of common necessaries; hundreds of thousands are in want of common comforts, Sir."

"Are there no prisons?" asked Scrooge.

"Plenty of prisons," said the gentleman, laying down the pen again.

"And the Union workhouses?" demanded Scrooge. "Are they still in operation?"

"They are. Still," returned the gentleman, "I wish I could say they were not."

"The Treadmill and the Poor Law are in full vigour then?" said Scrooge.

"Both very busy Sir."

"Oh! I was afraid, from what you said at first, that something had occurred, to stop them in their useful course," said Scrooge. "I'm very glad to hear it."

"Under the impression that they scarcely furnish Christian cheer of mind or body to the multitude," returned the gentleman, "a few of us are endeavouring to raise a fund to buy the Poor some meat and drink, and means of warmth. We choose this time because it is a time of all others when Want is keenly felt,and Abundance rejoices. What shall I put you down for?"

"Nothing," Scrooge replied.

"You wish to be anonymous?"

"I wish to be left alone," said Scrooge. "Since you ask me what I wish, gentlemen, that is my answer. I don't make merry myself at Christmas, and I can't afford to make idle people merry. I help to support the establishments I have mentioned—they cost enough—and those who are badly off must go there."

"Many can't go there; and many would rather die."

"If they would rather die," said Scrooge, "they had better do it, and decrease the surplus population. Besides; excuse me. I don't know that."

"But you might know it," observed the gentleman.

"It's not my business," Scrooge returned. "It's enough for a man to understand his own business, and not to interfere with other people's. Mine occupies me constantly. Good afternoon gentlemen!"

Seeing clearly that it would be useless to pursue their point, the gentlemen withdrew. Scrooge resumed his labors with an improved opinion of himself, and in a more facetious temper than was usual with him.

Meanwhile ^and darkness^ the fog thickened so, that people ran about with ~~flaring~~ links, proffering their services to go before ~~the~~ horses, and conduct them on their way. ^The ancient^ tower of a church ~~whose~~ gruff old bell was always ~~peeping~~ down at Scrooge out of a gothic window in the wall, became invisible and struck the hours and quarters in the clouds: with a tremulous vibration afterwards, as ~~though~~ if its teeth were chattering in its frozen head up there. The cold became intense. In the main street at the corner of the court ~~some~~ labourers were repairing the gas-pipes, and had lighted a great fire in a brazier, round which ~~a party of ragged men and boys were gathered~~ warming their hands and winking their eyes before the ~~blaze~~ in rapture. The water-plug being left in solitude, its overflowings sullenly ~~congealed~~ and turned to misanthropic ice. The brightness of the shops where holly sprigs and berries crackled in the ~~lamp~~ heat of the windows made pale faces ruddy as they passed. Poulterers' and grocers' trades became a splendid joke ^a glorious pageant^ ~~with which it was next to impossible to believe that~~ bargain and sale had anything to ~~do.~~ The Lord Mayor, in the ~~stronghold of the mighty Mansion House~~ gave orders to his fifty cooks and butlers ~~to~~ keep Christmas as a Lord Mayor's ~~household~~ should; and even the little tailor whom he had fined five shillings on the previous Monday for being drunk and bloodthirsty in the streets, stirred up to-morrow's pudding in his garret, while his lean wife ^and the baby^ sallied out to buy the beef.

Foggier ~~yet~~ and colder! ^Piercing, searching, biting cold.^ If the good Saint Dunstan had but nipped the Evil Spirit's nose ^with a touch of such weather as that^ indeed he would have roared to lusty purpose. The ~~owner of^ one scant ~~young~~ nose ~~gnawed and mumbled by the hungry cold, as bones are gnawed by dogs,~~ stooped down at Scrooge's ~~keyhole~~ to ~~regale~~ him with a Christmas carol; but at the first sound of

God bless you merry gentlemen! May nothing you dismay!

Scrooge seized the ruler with such ^energy^ ~~of action~~ that the singer fled in ~~terror,~~ leaving the keyhole to the fog and even more congenial ~~frost~~ ~~shutting up the counting house arrived.~~ With an ill-will, Scrooge ~~dismounted from his stool and~~ admitted the fact to the ~~expectant^ clerk in the ~~Tank~~: who instantly snuffed ~~his~~ candle out, and put on his hat.

"You'll want ^all day^ tomorrow, I suppose?" said Scrooge.

Meanwhile the fog and darkness thickened so, that people ran about with flaring links, proffering their services to go before horses in carriages, and conduct them on their way. The ancient tower of a church whose gruff old bell was always peeping slily down at Scrooge out of a gothic window in the wall, became invisible, and struck the hours and quarters in the clouds, with tremulous vibrations afterwards, as if its teeth were chattering in its frozen head up there. The cold became intense. In the main street at the corner of the court some labourers were repairing the gas pipes and had lighted a great fire in a brazier, round which a party of ragged men and boys were gathered, warming their hands and winking their eyes before the blaze in rapture. The water plug being left in solitude, its overflowings sullenly congealed and turned to misanthropic ice. The brightness of the shops where holly sprigs and berries crackled in the lamp-heat of the windows made pale faces ruddy as they passed. Poulterers' and grocers' trades became a splendid joke, a glorious pageant with which it was next to impossible to believe that such dull principles as bargain and sale had anything to do. The Lord Mayor in the stronghold of the awful Mansion House gave orders to his fifty cooks and butlers to keep Christmas as a Lord Mayor's household should; and even the little tailor whom he had fined five shillings on the previous Monday for being drunk and blood thirsty in the streets, stirred up tomorrow's pudding in his garret, while his lean wife and the baby sallied out to buy the beef.

Foggier yet, and colder! Piercing, searching, biting cold. If the good Saint Dunstan had but nipped the Evil Spirit's nose with a touch of such weather as that, instead of using his familiar weapons, then indeed he would have roared to lusty purpose. The owner of one scant young nose, gnawed and mumbled by the hungry cold, as bones are gnawed by dogs, stooped down at Scrooge's keyhole, to regale him with a Christmas carol: but at the first sound of

God bless you merry gentleman! May nothing you dismay!

Scrooge seized the ruler with such energy of action that the singer fled in terror, leaving the keyhole to the fog and even more congenial frost.

At length the hour of shutting up the counting house arrived. With an ill will, Scrooge dismounted from his stool, and tacitly admitted the fact to the expectant clerk in the tank, who instantly snuffed his candle out, and put on his hat.

"You'll want all day tomorrow, I suppose?" said Scrooge.

8

"If quite convenient, Sir."

"It's not convenient," said Scrooge, "and it's not fair. If I was to stop half-a-crown for it, you'd think yourself ill-used, I'll be bound?"

The clerk smiled faintly.

"And yet," said Scrooge, "you don't think me ill-used, when I pay a day's wages for no work."

The clerk observed that it was only once a year.

"A poor excuse for picking a man's pocket every twenty-fifth of December!" said Scrooge, buttoning his great-coat to the chin. "But I suppose you must have the whole day. Be here all the earlier next morning!"

The clerk promised that he would; and Scrooge walked out with a growl. The office was closed in a twinkling, and the clerk, with the long ends of his white comforter dangling below his waist (for he boasted no great coat), went down a slide on Cornhill, at the end of a lane of boys, twenty times, in honor of its being Christmas Eve, and then ran home to Camden Town as hard as he could pelt, to play at blindman's buff.

Scrooge took his melancholy dinner in his usual melancholy tavern; and having read all the newspapers, and beguiled the rest of the evening with his banker's-book, went home to bed. He lived in chambers which had once belonged to his deceased partner. They were a gloomy suite of rooms, in a lowering pile of building up a yard, where it had so little business to be, that one could scarcely help fancying it must have run there when it was a young house, playing at hide and seek with other houses; and have forgotten the way out again. It was old enough now, and dreary enough, for nobody lived in it but Scrooge, the other rooms being all let out as offices. The yard was so dark that even Scrooge, who knew its every stone, was fain to grope with his hands. The fog and frost so hung about the black old gateway of the house, that it seemed as if the Genius of the Weather sat in mournful meditation on the threshold.

Now, it is a fact that there was nothing at all particular about the knocker on the door, except that it was very large. It is also a fact that Scrooge had seen it, night and morning, during his whole residence in that place. Scrooge had as little of what is called fancy about him as any man in the city of London, even including — which is a bold word — the corporation, aldermen, and livery. Let it also be borne in mind that Scrooge had not bestowed one thought on Marley, since his last mention of his seven-years' dead partner that afternoon. And then let any man explain to me, if he can, how it happened that Scrooge, having his key in the lock of the door, saw in the knocker, without its undergoing any intermediate process of change — not a knocker, but

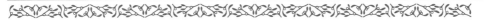

"If quite convenient, Sir."

"It's not convenient," said Scrooge, "and it's not fair. If I was to stop half a crown for it, you'd think yourself ill-used, I'll be bound?"

The clerk smiled faintly.

"And yet," said Scrooge, you don't think *me* ill-used, when I pay a day's wages for no work."

The clerk observed that it was only once a year.

"A poor excuse for picking a man's pocket every twenty fifth of December!" said Scrooge, buttoning his great coat to the chin. "But I suppose you must have the whole day. Be here all the earlier next morning!"

The clerk promised that he would; and Scrooge walked out, with a growl. The office was closed in a twinkling, and the clerk with the long ends of his white comforter dangling below his waist (for he boasted no great coat), went down a slide on Cornhill, at the end of a lane of boys, twenty times in honour of its being Christmas Eve, and then ran home to Camden Town as hard as he could pelt, to play at blindman's buff.

Scrooge took his melancholy dinner in his usual melancholy tavern; and having read all the newspapers, and beguiled the rest of the evening with his banker's-book, went home to bed. He lived in chambers which had once belonged to his deceased partner. They were a gloomy suite of rooms in a lowering pile of building up a yard where it had so little business to be, that one could scarcely help fancying it must have run there, when it was a young house, playing at hide and seek with other houses; and have forgotten the way out again. It was old enough now, and dreary enough, for nobody lived in it but Scrooge: the other rooms being all let out as offices. The yard was so dark that even Scrooge, who knew its every stone, was fain to grope with his hands. The fog and frost so hung about the black old gateway of the house, that it seemed as if the Genius of the Weather sat in mournful meditation on the threshold.

Now, it is a fact, that there was nothing at all particular about the knocker on the door— except that it was very large. It is also a fact that Scrooge had seen it, night and morning during his whole residence in that place; also that Scrooge had as little of what is called fancy about him as any man in the City of London; even including—which is a bold word—the corporation, aldermen, and livery. Let it also be borne in mind that Scrooge had not bestowed one thought on Marley since his last mention of his seven-years dead partner that afternoon. And then let any man explain to me if he can, how it happened that Scrooge, having his key in the lock of the door, saw in the knocker, without its undergoing any intermediate process of change—not a knocker, but

9

Marley's face. It was not in impenetrable
shadow as the other objects in the yard were, but had a dismal light
about it, like a bad lobster in a dark cellar. It was not angry or
ferocious, but looked at Scrooge as Marley used to look: with ghostly spectacles turned up on its ghostly forehead.
The hair was curiously stirred, as if
by breath or hot air, though the eyes were wide open they were
perfectly motionless. That, and its livid color, made it horrible; but its
horror seemed to be in spite of the face and beyond its control, rather than a part of its own expression.

As Scrooge looked fixedly at this phenomenon, it was a knocker
again.

To say that he was not startled, or that his blood was
not conscious of a terrible sensation to which it had been a stranger from infancy,
would be untrue. But he put his hand upon the key he had relinquished;
turned it sturdily; walked in, and lighted his candle.

He did pause, with a moment's irresolution, before he shut the
door, and he did look cautiously behind it first, as if he half-expected to be
terrified with the sight of Marley's pigtail sticking out into the hall.
But there was nothing on the back of the door, except the screws and
nuts that held the knocker on; so he said "Pooh Pooh!" and
closed it with a bang.

The sound resounded through the house, like thunder. Every room
above, and every cask in the wine-merchant's cellars below, appeared to have
a separate peal of echoes of its own. Scrooge was not a man to be
frightened by echoes. He fastened the door; and walked across the hall,
and up the stairs - slowly too - trimming his candle as he went.

You may talk vaguely about driving a coach and six up a good flight of
stairs, or through a bad young act of Parliament; but I mean to
say you might have got a hearse up that staircase, and
taken it broadwise, with the splinter-bar towards the wall, and the
door towards the balustrades - and done it easy. There was plenty of width
for that, and room to spare; which is perhaps the reason why Scrooge thought he saw a locomotive hearse going on before him in the gloom. Half a dozen gas lamps out of the street
wouldn't have lighted too well; so you may suppose that it was
pretty dark, with Scrooge's dip.

Up Scrooge went, not caring a button for that. darkness is
cheap, and Scrooge liked it. But before he shut his heavy door, he walked
through his rooms to see that all was right. He had just enough recollection

Marley's face.

Marley's face. It was not in impenetrable shadow as the other objects in the yard were, but had a dismal light about it, like a bad lobster in a dark cellar. It was not angry, or ferocious, but looked at Scrooge as Marley used to look: with ghostly spectacles turned up on its ghostly forehead. The hair was curiously stirred, as if by breath or hot air, and though the eyes were wide open, they were perfectly motionless. That, and its livid color, made it horrible; but its horror seemed to be in spite of the face and beyond its control, rather than a part of its own expression.

As Scrooge looked fixedly at this phenomenon, it was a knocker again.

To say that he was not startled, or that his blood was not conscious of a terrible sensation to which it had been a stranger from infancy, would be untrue. But he put his hand upon the key he had relinquished; turned it sturdily; walked in; and lighted his candle.

He *did* pause, with a moment's irresolution, before he shut the door, and he *did* look cautiously behind it first, as if he half-expected to be terrified with the sight of Marley's pigtail sticking out into the hall. But there was nothing on the back of the door, except the screws and nuts that held the knocker on; so he said "Pooh. Pooh!" and closed it with a bang.

The sound resounded through the house, like thunder. Every room above, and every cask in the wine-merchant's cellars below, appeared to have a separate peal of echoes of its own. Scrooge was not a man to be frightened by echoes. He fastened the door, and walked across the hall, and up the stairs—slowly too—trimming his candle as he went.

You may talk vaguely about driving a coach and six up a good old flight of stairs or through a bad young act of Parliament; but I mean to say you might have got a Hearse up that staircase, and taken it broadwise, with the splinter-bar towards the wall, and the door towards the balustrades—and done it easy. There was plenty of width for that, and room to spare; which is perhaps the reason why Scrooge thought he saw a locomotive hearse going on before him in the gloom. Half a dozen gas lamps out of the street wouldn't have lighted the entry too well; so you may suppose that it was pretty dark with Scrooge's dip.

Up Scrooge went, not caring a button for that: darkness is cheap, and Scrooge liked it. But before he shut his heavy door, he walked through his rooms to see that all was right. He had just enough recollection of the face to desire to do that.

Sitting-room, bedroom, lumber room. All as they should be: nobody under the table, nobody under the sofa; a small fire in the grate; and the little saucepan of gruel (Scrooge had a cold in his head) upon the hob. Nobody under the bed; nobody in the closet; nobody in his dressing gown, which was hanging up in a suspicious attitude against the wall. Lumber-room as usual. Old fire-guard, old shoes, his hat-baskets washing-stand on three legs, and a poker.

Quite satisfied, he closed his door, and locked himself in — double-locked himself in: which was not his custom. Thus secured against surprise, he took off his cravat; put on his dressing gown and slippers, and his nightcap; and sat down before the fire to take his gruel.

It was a very low fire indeed; nothing on such a bitter night. He was obliged to sit close to it, and brood over it, before he could extract the least sensation of warmth from such a handful of fuel. The fire-place was an old one, built by some Dutch merchant, long ago, and paved all round with quaint Dutch tiles, designed to illustrate the Scriptures. There were Cains and Abels, Pharoahs' daughters, Queens of Sheba, Angelic messengers descending through the air on clouds like feather-beds, Abrahams, Belshazzars, Apostles putting off to sea in butter-boats, hundreds of figures, to attract his thoughts; and yet that face of Marley, seven years dead, came like the ancient Prophet's rod, and swallowed up the whole. If each smooth tile had been a blank at first, with power to shape some picture on its surface from the disjointed fragments of his thoughts, there would have been a copy of old Marley's head on every one.

"Humbug!" said Scrooge; and walked across the room.

After several turns, he sat down again. As he threw his head back in his chair, his glance happened to rest upon a bell, that hung in the room, and communicated for some purpose now forgotten with a chamber in the highest story of the building. It was with great astonishment, and with a strange, inexplicable dread, that as he looked, he saw this bell begin to swing. It swung so softly in the outset that it scarcely made a sound; but soon it rang out loudly, and so did every bell in the house.

This might have lasted half a minute, or a minute, but it seemed an hour. The bells ceased as they had begun, together. They were succeeded by a clanking noise, deep down below; as if some person were dragging

of the face to desire to do that.

Sitting-room, bedroom, lumber-room. All as they should be. Nobody under the table, nobody under the sofa; a small fire in the grate; spoon and basin ready; and the little saucepan of gruel (Scrooge had a cold in his head) upon the hob. Nobody under the bed; nobody in the closet; nobody in his dressing gown, which was hanging up in a suspicious attitude against the wall. Lumber-room as usual. Old fire-guard, old shoes, two fish-baskets, washing-stand on three legs, and a poker.

Quite satisfied, he closed his door, and locked himself in—double-locked himself in: which was not his custom. Thus secured against surprise, he took off his cravat; put on his dressing gown and slippers, and his nightcap; and sat down before the fire to take his gruel.

It was a very low fire indeed; nothing on such a bitter night. He was obliged to sit close to it, and brood over it, before he could extract the least sensation of warmth from such a handfull of fuel. The fire-place was an old one, built by some Dutch merchant, long ago, and paved all round with quaint Dutch tiles, designed to illustrate the Scriptures. There were Cains and Abels, Pharaoh's daughters, Queens of Sheba, angelic messengers descending through the air on clouds like feather beds: Abrahams, Belshazzars, Apostles putting off to sea in butter-boats, hundreds of figures, to attract his thoughts; and yet that face of Marley seven years dead, came like the ancient Prophet's rod, and swallowed up the whole. If each smooth tile had been a blank at first, with power to shape some picture on its surface from the disjointed fragments of his thoughts, there would have been a copy of old Marley's head on every one.

"Humbug!" said Scrooge; and walked across the room.

After several turns, he sat down again. As he threw his head back in the chair, his glance happened to rest upon a bell—a disused bell—that hung in the room, and communicated for some purpose now forgotten with a chamber in the highest story of the building. It was with great astonishment, and with a strange, inexplicable dread, that as he looked, he saw this bell begin to swing. It swung so softly in the outset that it scarcely made a sound; but soon it rang out loud. And so did every bell in the house.

This might have lasted half a minute, or a minute, but it seemed an hour. The bells ceased as they had begun, together. They were succeeded by a clanking noise, deep down below; as if some person were dragging

a heavy chain on the cask in the wine merchant's cellar. Scrooge then remembered
to have heard that ghosts in haunted houses were described as dragging chains. The cellar-door flew open with a booming sound, and then he heard the
noise much louder, on the floors below; then coming up
the stairs; then coming straight towards his door.

"It's humbug still!" said Scrooge. "I won't believe it.

His colour changed though, as it came on through the heavy door, and
passed into the room before his eyes. Upon its coming in, the
dying flame leaped up, as though it cried "I know him! Marley's Ghost!" and
fell again.

The same face; the very same. Marley in his pigtail, usual
waistcoat, tights, and boots; the tassels on the latter, bristling like his
pigtail, and and his coat-skirts, and the hair upon his head. The chain he drew was clasped about his middle. It was long, and
wound about him like a tail; it was made (for Scrooge observed it closely) of cash-boxes, keys, padlocks,
ledgers, deeds, and heavy purses wrought in steel. His body was transparent;
so that Scrooge observing him, and looking through his waistcoat, could
see the two buttons on his coat behind. Scrooge had often heard it said that
Marley had no bowels, but had never believed it until now.

No, nor did he believe it even now. Though he looked the phantom
through and through, and saw it standing before him; though he felt the chilling influence of its
death-cold eyes; and marked the very texture of the folded kerchief
bound about its head and chin, which wrapper he had
not observed before; he was still incredulous, and fought against his
senses.

"How now!" said Scrooge, caustic and cold as ever. "What do you want
with me?"

"Much!" — Marley's voice, no doubt about it.

"Who are you?"

"Ask me who I was."

"Who were you then?" said raising his voice. "You're particular for a shade." He was
going to say "to a shade," but substituted this, as more appropriate.

"In life I was your partner, Jacob Marley."

"Can you — can you sit down?" asked Scrooge, looking doubtfully at him.

"I can."

"Do it then."

Scrooge asked the question, because he didn't know whether a ghost

a heavy chain over the casks in the wine merchant's cellar. Scrooge then remembered to have heard that ghosts in Haunted Houses were described as dragging chains.

The cellar-door flew open with a booming sound, and then he heard the noise much louder, on the floors below; then coming up the stairs; then coming straight towards his door.

"It's humbug still!" said Scrooge. "I won't believe it."

His colour changed though, when, without a pause, it came on through the heavy door, and passed into the room before his eyes. Upon its coming in, the dying flame leaped up, as though it cried "I know him! Marley's Ghost!" and fell again.

The same face: the very same. Marley in his pigtail, usual waistcoat, tights, and boots; the tassels on the latter, bristling like his pigtail, and his coat-skirts, and the hair upon his head. The chain he drew was clasped about his middle. It was long, and wound about him like a tail; and it was made (for Scrooge observed it closely) of cash-boxes, keys, padlocks, ledgers, deeds, and heavy purses wrought in steel. His body was transparent, so that Scrooge, observing him, and looking through his waistcoat, could see the two buttons on his coat behind.

Scrooge had often heard it said that Marley had no bowels, but he had never believed it until now.

No, nor did he believe it, even now. Though he looked the phantom through and through, and saw it standing before him; though he felt the chilling influence of its death-cold eyes; and marked the very texture of the folded kerchief bound about its head and chin; which wrapper he had not observed before; he was still incredulous, and fought against his senses.

"How now!" said Scrooge, caustic and cold as ever. "What do you want with me?"

"Much!"—Marley's voice, no doubt about it.

"Who are you?"

"Ask me who I *was*."

"Who *were* you then?" said Scrooge, raising his voice. "You're particular—for a shade." He was going to say "*to* a shade," but substituted this, as more appropriate.

"In life I was your partner; Jacob Marley."

"Can you—can you sit down?" asked Scrooge, looking doubtfully at him.

"I can."

"Do it then."

Scrooge asked the question, because he didn't know whether a ghost so transparent might find himself in a condition to take a chair, and felt that in the event of its being impossible it might involve the necessity of an embarrassing explanation. But the ghost sat down on the opposite side of the fireplace, as if he were quite used to it.

"You don't believe in me," observed the Ghost.

"I don't," said Scrooge.

"What evidence would you have of my reality beyond that of your senses?"

"I don't know," said Scrooge.

"Why do you doubt your senses?"

"Because," said Scrooge, "a little thing affects them. A slight disorder of the stomach makes them cheats. You may be an undigested bit of beef, a blot of mustard, a crumb of cheese, a fragment of an underdone potato. There's more of gravy than of grave about you, whatever you are!"

Scrooge was not much in the habit of cracking jokes, nor did he feel, in his heart, by any means waggish then. The truth is, that he tried to be smart, as a means of distracting his own attention, and keeping down his terror; for the spectre's voice disturbed the very marrow in his bones.

To sit staring at those fixed glazed eyes in silence for a moment would play, Scrooge felt, the very deuce with him. There was something very awful, too, in the spectre's being provided with an infernal atmosphere of its own. Scrooge could not feel it himself, but this was clearly the case; for though the ghost sat perfectly motionless, its hair, and skirts, and tassels, were still agitated as by the hot vapour from an oven.

"You see this toothpick," said Scrooge, returning quickly to the charge, for the reason just assigned: and wishing, though it were for a second, to divert the vision's stony gaze from himself.

"I do," replied the Ghost.

"You're not looking at it," said Scrooge.

"But I see it," said the Ghost, "notwithstanding."

"Well!" returned Scrooge. "I have but to swallow this, and be for the rest of my days persecuted by a legion of goblins, all of my own creation. Humbug, I tell you. humbug!"

At this the Spirit raised a frightful cry, and shook its chain with such a dismal and appalling noise, that Scrooge held on tight to his chair, to keep himself from falling in a swoon. But how much greater was his horror, when the Phantom taking off the bandage round its head, as if it were too

transparent might find himself in a condition to take a chair; and felt that in the event of its being impossible it might involve the necessity of an embarrassing explanation. But the ghost sat down, on the opposite side of the fireplace, as if he were quite used to it.

"You don't believe in me," observed the Ghost.

"I don't," said Scrooge.

"What evidence would you have of my reality, beyond that of your senses?"

"I don't know," said Scrooge.

"Why do you doubt your senses?"

"Because," said Scrooge, "a little thing affects them. A slight disorder of the stomach makes them cheats. You may be an undigested bit of beef, a blot of mustard, a crumb of cheese, a fragment of an underdone potato. There's more of gravy than of grave about you, whatever you are!"

Scrooge was not much in the habit of cracking jokes, nor did he feel, in his heart, by any means waggish then. The truth is that he tried to be smart, as a means of distracting his own attention and keeping down his terror; for the spectre's voice disturbed the very marrow in his bones.

To sit staring at those fixed, glazed eyes, in silence for a moment, would play, Scrooge felt, the very deuce with him. There was something very awful too in the spectre's being provided with an infernal atmosphere of its own. Scrooge could not feel it himself, but this was clearly the case, for though the Ghost sat perfectly motionless, its hair, and skirts, and tassels were still agitated as by the hot vapour from an oven.

"You see this toothpick—" said Scrooge: returning quickly to the charge, for the reason just assigned: and wishing, though it were only for a second, to divert the vision's stony gaze from himself.

"I do," replied the Ghost.

"You are not looking at it," said Scrooge.

"But I see it," said the Ghost, "notwithstanding."

"Well!" returned Scrooge, "I have but to swallow this, and be for the rest of my days, persecuted by a legion of goblins, all of my own creation. Humbug, I tell you—humbug!"

At this, the Spirit raised a frightful cry, and shook its chain with such a dismal and appalling noise, that Scrooge held on tight to his chair, to save himself from falling in a swoon. But how much greater was his horror, when the Phantom, taking off the bandage round its head, as if it were too warned to near ... -doors, its ... lower jaw ... chopped down upon its breast!

Scrooge fell upon his knees, and clasped his hands before his face.

"Mercy!" he said. "Dreadful ... apparition, why do you trouble me!"

"Man of the worldly mind!" replied the ... Ghost. "Do you believe in me or not?"

"I do," said Scrooge. "I must. But why do spirits ... earth, ... the first returned, "that the Spirit within him should walk abroad among his fellow-men, and travel far and wide. And if that Spirit goes not forth in life, it is condemned to do so after death. ... Wanderings through the world, oh woe is me! — and witness what it cannot share, but might have ... shared ... and turned to ... of happiness!"

... again ... the Spectre raised a cry, and shook its chain, and wrung its ... hands.

"You are fettered," said Scrooge, trembling. ... "Tell me why?"

"I wear the chain I forged in life," replied the Ghost. "I made it link by link, and yard by yard; I ... girded it ... on of my own free will, and of my own free-will I wore it. Is it's pattern strange to you?"

Scrooge trembled more and more.

"Or would you know," pursued the Ghost, "the weight and length of ... you bear yourself? It was full as heavy and as long as this, seven christmas Eves ago. You have laboured on it since. It is a ponderous chain!"

Scrooge ... him on the floor ... in the expectation of finding himself surrounded by some fifty or sixty fathoms of iron cable; but he could see nothing.

"Jacob," he said, imploringly. "old Jacob Marley, tell me more. ... Jacob."

"I have none to give," the Ghost replied. "It comes from other regions, wherever Scrooge, and is ... by other ministers, ... nor can I tell you what I would. A very little more is all permitted to us. I may not rest, I may not stay, I may not linger anywhere. My spirit never walked beyond our counting-house — mark me! — in life my spirit never ... ; and weary journeys lie before me!"

It was ... a habit with Scrooge, whenever he became thoughtful

warm to wear in-doors, its lower jaw dropped down upon its breast!

Scrooge fell upon his knees, and clasped his hands before his face.

"Mercy!" he said. "Dreadful apparition, why do you trouble me?"

"Man of the worldly mind!" replied the Ghost, "do you believe in me or not?"

"I do," said Scrooge. "I must. But why do spirits walk the earth, and why to me?"

"It is required of every man," the Ghost returned, "that the spirit within him should walk abroad among his fellow-men, and travel far and wide. And if that spirit goes not forth in life it is condemned to do so, after death. It is doomed to wander through the world, oh woe is me!—and witness what it can no longer share, but might have shared on earth, and turned to Happiness!"

Again the spectre raised a cry, and shook its chain, and wrung its shadowy hands.

"You are fettered," said Scrooge, trembling. "Tell me why?"

"I wear the chain I forged in Life," replied the Ghost. "I made it link by link, and yard by yard; I girded it on, of my own free will, and of my own free will I wore it. Is it's pattern strange to *you?*"

Scrooge trembled more and more.

"Or would you know," pursued the Ghost, "the weight and length of the strong coil you wear yourself? It was full as heavy and as long as this, seven Christmas Eves ago. You have laboured on it, since. It is a ponderous chain!"

Scrooge glanced about him on the floor, in the expectation of finding himself surrounded by some fifty or sixty fathoms of iron cable: but he could see nothing.

"Jacob," he said, imploringly. "Old Jacob Marley, tell me more. Speak comfort to me, Jacob!"

"I have none to give," the Ghost replied. "It comes from other regions, Ebenezer Scrooge, and is conveyed by other ministers, to other kinds of men. Nor can I tell you what I would. A very little more, is all permitted to me. I may not rest, I may not stay, I may not linger anywhere. My spirit never walked beyond our counting-house—mark me!—in life my spirit never roved beyond the narrow limits of our money-changing hole; and weary journeys lie before me!"

It was a habit with Scrooge whenever he became thoughtful

who put his hands in his pockets. 14 Pondering on what the Ghost had said, he did so now but without raising lifting up his eyes, or getting off his knees.

"You must have been very slow about it, Jacob," Scrooge observed — in a business-like manner, in deference

"Slow!" the Ghost repeated.

"Seven years dead?" mused Scrooge. "And travelling all the time?"

"The whole time," said the Ghost. "No rest, no peace. Incessant torture of remorse."

"You travel fast?" said Scrooge.

"On the wings of the wind," replied the Ghost.

"You might have got over a great quantity of ground in seven years," said Scrooge.

The Ghost on hearing this, set up another cry, and clanked his chain so hideous in the dead silence of the night, that the Ward would have been justified in indicting him for a nuisance.

"Oh! captive, bound, and double-ironed," cried the phantom "not to know, that ages of incessant labour by immortal creatures for this earth, must pass into eternity before the good of which it is susceptible is all developed — not to know that any christian spirit working kindly in its little sphere, whatever it may be, will find its mortal life too short for its vast means of usefulness — not to know that no space of regret can make amends for one life's opportunity misused! Yet such was I! Oh! Such was I!"

"You were always a good man of business, Jacob," faltered Scrooge, who now began to apply this to himself.

"Business!" cried the Ghost, wringing its hands again. "Mankind was my business. The common welfare was my business; charity, mercy, forbearance, and benevolence, were all my business. The dealings of my trade were but a drop of water in the comprehensive ocean of my business!"

It held up its chain at arm's length, as if that were the cause of all its unavailing grief; and flung it heavily upon the ground again.

"At this time of the rolling year," the spectre said, "I suffer most. Why did I walk through crowds of fellow-beings with my eyes turned down, and never raise them to that blessed star which led the wise men to a poor abode? Were there no poor homes to which its light would have conducted me!"

Scrooge was very much dismayed to hear the spectre going on at

to put his hands in his breeches pockets. Pondering on what the Ghost had said, he did so now, but without lifting up his eyes, or getting off his knees.

"You must have been very slow about it, Jacob," Scrooge observed—in a business-like manner, though with humility and deference.

"Slow!" the Ghost repeated.

"Seven years dead," mused Scrooge. "And travelling all the time?"

"The whole time," said the Ghost. "No rest, no peace. Incessant torture of remorse."

"You travel fast?" said Scrooge.

"On the wings of the wind," replied the Ghost.

"You might have got over a great quantity of ground in seven years," said Scrooge.

The Ghost, on hearing this, set up another cry, and clanked his chain so hideously in the dead silence of the night, that the Ward would have been justified in indicting him for a nuisance.

"Oh! captive, bound and double-ironed," cried the phantom, "not to know, that ages of incessant labour by immortal creatures, for this earth must pass into eternity before the good of which it is susceptible is all developed not to know that any Christian spirit working kindly in its little sphere, whatever it may be, will find its mortal life too short for its vast means of usefulness—not to know that no space of regret can make amends for one Life's opportunities misused! Yet such was I! Oh! such was I!"

"But you were always a good man of business, Jacob," faltered Scrooge who now began to apply this to himself.

"Business!" cried the Ghost, wringing its hands again. "Mankind was my business. The common welfare was my business; charity, mercy, forbearance, and benevolence, were, all, my business. The dealings of my trade were but a drop of water in the comprehensive Ocean of my business!"

It held up its chain at arm's length as if that were the cause of all its unavailing grief; and flung it heavily upon the ground again.

"At this time of the rolling year," the spectre said, "I suffer most: why did I walk through crowds of fellow-beings with my eyes turned down, and never raise them to that blessed star which led the wise men to a poor abode? Were there no poor homes to which its light would have conducted *me!*"

Scrooge was very much dismayed to hear the spectre going on at this rate; and began to quake exceedingly.

"Hear me!" cried the Ghost. "My time is nearly gone."

"I will," said Scrooge. "But don't be hard upon me! Don't be flowery, Jacob! Pray!"

"How it is that I appear before you in a shape that you can see, I may not tell. I have sat invisible beside you many and many a day."

It was not an agreeable idea. Scrooge shivered, and wiped the perspiration from his brow.

"You will be haunted," resumed the Ghost, "by Three Spirits."

"Is that the chance and hope you mentioned, Jacob?" he demanded, in a faltering voice.

"It is."

"I — I think I'd rather not," said Scrooge.

"Without their visits," said the Ghost, "you cannot hope to shun the path I tread. Expect the first tomorrow, when the bell tolls one."

"Couldn't I take 'em all at once, and have it over, Jacob?" hinted Scrooge.

"Expect the second, on the next night at the same hour. The third on the next night when the same hour. Look to see me no more; and look that, for your own sake, you remember what has passed between us!"

When it had said these words, the spectre took its wrapper from the table, and bound it round its head, as before. Scrooge knew this, by the smart sound its teeth made, when the jaws were brought together by the bandage. He raised his eyes again, and found his visitor confronting him in an erect attitude, with his chain wound over and about his arm.

The apparition walked backward from him; and at every step it took, the window raised itself a little; so that when the spectre reached it, it was wide open. It beckoned Scrooge to approach, which he did. When they were within two paces of each other, Marley's Ghost held up its hand, warning him to come no nearer. Scrooge stopped.

Not so much in obedience, as in surprise and fear: for on the raising of the hand, he became sensible of confused noises in the

this rate, and began to quake exceedingly.

"Hear me!" cried the Ghost. "My time is nearly gone."

"I will," said Scrooge. "But don't be hard upon me! Don't be flowery, Jacob! Pray!"

"How it is that I appear before you in a shape that you can see, I may not tell. I have sat invisible beside you, many and many a day."

It was not an agreeable idea. Scrooge shivered, and wiped the perspiration from his brow.

"That is no light part of my penance," pursued the Ghost. "I am here tonight to warn you that you have yet a chance and hope of escaping my fate. A chance and hope of my procuring, Ebenezer."

"You were always a good friend to me," said Scrooge. "Thank'ee!"

"You will be haunted," resumed the Ghost, "by three spirits."

Scrooge's countenance fell, almost as low as the Ghost's had done.

"Is that the chance and favor that you mentioned, Jacob?" he demanded in a faltering voice.

"It is."

"I—I think I'd rather not," said Scrooge.

"Without their visits," said the Ghost, "you cannot hope to shun the path I tread. Expect the first tomorrow, when the bell tolls one."

"Couldn't I take 'em all at once, and have it over, Jacob?" hinted Scrooge.

"Expect the second on the next night at the same hour. The third upon the next night at the same hour. Look to see me no more; and look that for your own sake you remember what has passed between us!"

When it had said these words, the spectre took its wrapper from the table, and bound it round its head, as before. Scrooge knew this, by the smart sound its teeth made, when the jaws were brought together by the bandage. He ventured to raise his eyes again, and found his supernatural visitor confronting him in an erect attitude, with its chain wound over and about its arm.

The apparition walked backward from him; and at every step it took, the window raised itself a little; so that when the spectre reached it, it was wide open. It beckoned Scrooge to approach, which he did. When they were within two paces of each other, Marley's Ghost held up its hand, warning him to come no nearer. Scrooge stopped.

Not so much in obedience, as in surprise and fear: for on the raising of the hand, he became sensible of confused noises in the air; incoherent sounds of lamentation and regret; wailings inexpressibly sorrowful and self-accusatory. The Spectre, after listening for a moment, joined in the mournful dirge; and floated out upon the bleak, dark night.

Scrooge followed to the window: desperate in his curiosity. He looked out.

The air was filled with phantoms, wandering hither and thither in restless haste, and moaning as they went. Every one of them wore chains like Marley's Ghost; some few were linked together; none were free. Many had been personally known to Scrooge in their lives. He had been quite familiar with one old ghost in a white waistcoat, with a monstrous iron safe attached to his ancle, who cried piteously at being unable to assist a wretched woman with an infant, whom he saw below, upon a door-step. The misery with them all was, clearly, that they sought to interfere, for good, in human matters, and had lost the power for ever.

Whether these creatures faded into mist, or mist enshrouded them, he could not tell. But they, and their spirit voices faded together; and the night became as it had been when he walked home.

Scrooge closed the window, and examined the door by which the Ghost had entered. It was double-locked, as he had locked it with his own hands, and the bolts were undisturbed. He tried to say "Humbug!" but stopped at the first syllable. And being, from the emotion he had undergone, or the fatigues of the day, or his glimpse of the Invisible World, or the dull conversation of the Ghost, or the lateness of the hour, much in need of repose; went straight to bed, without undressing, and fell asleep upon the instant.

air; incoherent sounds of lamentation and regret; wailings inexpressibly sorrowful and self-accusatory. The spectre after listening for a moment, joined in the mournful dirge; and floated out upon the bleak, dark night.

Scrooge followed to the window: desperate in his curiosity. He looked out.

The air was filled with phantoms, wandering hither and thither in restless haste, and moaning as they went. Every one of them wore chains like Marley's Ghost; some few (they might be guilty governments) were linked together; none were free. Many had been personally known to Scrooge in their lives. He had been quite familiar with one old ghost in a white waistcoat, with a monstrous iron safe attached to its ancle, who cried piteously at being unable to assist a wretched woman with an infant, whom he saw below, upon a door-step. The misery with them all was, clearly, that they sought to interfere, for good, in human matters, and had lost the power for ever.

Whether these creatures faded into mist, or mist enshrouded them, he could not tell. But they and their spirit-voices faded together; and the night became as it had been when he walked home.

Scrooge closed the window, and examined the door by which the Ghost had entered. It was double-locked as he had locked it with his own hands, and the bolts were undisturbed. He tried to say "Humbug!" but stopped at the first syllable. And being—from the emotion he had undergone, or the fatigues of the day, or his glimpse of the Invisible World, or the dull conversation of the Ghost, or the lateness of the hour—much in need of repose, went straight to bed, without undressing, and fell asleep upon the instant.

Stave II.

The First of The Three Spirits.

When Scrooge awoke, it was so dark, that looking out of bed he could scarcely distinguish the transparent window from the opaque walls of his chamber. He was trying to pierce the darkness with his ferret eyes, when the chimes of a neighbouring church struck the four quarters. So he listened for the hour.

To his great astonishment, the heavy bell went on from six to seven, and from seven to eight, and regularly up to twelve, then stopped. Twelve! It was past two when he went to bed. The clock was wrong. An icicle must have got into the works. Twelve!

He touched the spring of his repeater, to correct this most preposterous clock. Its rapid little pulse beat twelve; and stopped.

"Why, it isn't possible," said Scrooge, "that I can have slept through a whole day and far into another night. It isn't possible that anything has happened to the sun, and this is twelve at noon!"

The idea being an alarming one, he scrambled out of bed, and groped his way to the window. He was obliged to rub the frost off with the sleeve of his dressing-gown before he could see anything; and could see very little then. All that he could make out was, that it was still very foggy and extremely cold, and that there was no noise of people running to and fro and making a great stir, as there unquestionably would have been if the night had beaten off the bright Day, and taken possession of the world. This was a great relief, because "three days after sight of this First of Exchange pay to Mr Ebenezer Scrooge or his order" and so forth, would have become a mere United States security if there were no days to count by.

Scrooge went to bed again, and thought, and thought, and thought it over and over and over, and could make nothing of it. The more he thought, the more perplexed he was; and the more he endeavoured not to think, the more he thought. Marley's Ghost bothered him exceedingly. Every time he resolved within himself, after mature inquiry that it was all a dream, his mind flew back again, like a strong spring released, to its first position, and presented the same problem to be worked all through. "Was it a dream or not?"

Scrooge lay in this state until the chimes had gone three quarters more, when he remembered, on a sudden, that the Ghost had

STAVE II.

The First of the Three Spirits.

When Scrooge awoke, it was so dark, that looking out of bed he could scarcely distinguish, the transparent window from the opaque walls of his chamber. He was endeavouring to pierce the darkness with his ferret eyes, when the chimes of a neighbouring church struck the four quarters. So he listened for the hour.

To his great astonishment the heavy bell went on from six to seven, and from seven to eight, and regularly up to twelve; then stopped. Twelve! It was past Two when he went to bed. The clock was wrong. An icicle must have got into the works. Twelve!

He touched the spring of his repeater, to correct this most preposterous clock. Its rapid little pulse beat Twelve; and stopped.

"Why, it isn't possible," said Scrooge, "that I can have slept through a whole day and far into another night. It isn't possible that anything has happened to the sun, and this is twelve at noon!"

The idea being an alarming one he scrambled out of bed, and groped his way to the window. He was obliged to rub the frost off with the sleeve of his dressing-gown before he could see anything; and could see very little then. All he could make out, was, that it was still very foggy and extremely cold, and that there was no noise of people running to and fro, and making a great stir, as there unquestionably would have been if night had beaten off bright Day, and taken possession of the world. This was a great relief, because "sixty days after sight pay to me my order," and so forth, would have become a mere United States' security if there were no days to count by.

Scrooge went to bed again, and thought and thought; and thought it over and over and over, and could make nothing of it. The more he thought, the more perplexed he was; and the more he endeavoured not to think, the more he thought. Marley's Ghost bothered him exceedingly. Every time he resolved within himself, after mature enquiry, that it was all a dream, his mind flew back again, like a strong spring released, to its first position, and presented the same problem to be worked all through, "Was it a dream or not?"

Scrooge lay in this state, until the chimes had gone three quarters more; when he remembered on a sudden, that the Ghost had warned him of a visitation when the bell tolled out. He resolved to lie awake until the hour was past; and considering that he could no more go to sleep than go to Heaven, this was perhaps the wisest resolution in his power.

The quarter was so long, that he was more than once convinced he must have sunk into a doze unconsciously, and missed the clock. At length it broke upon his listening ear.

"Ding Dong!"

"A quarter past!" said Scrooge, counting.

"Ding Dong!"

"Half past!" said Scrooge.

"Ding Dong!"

"A quarter to it," said Scrooge.

"Ding Dong!"

"The hour itself," said Scrooge triumphantly, "and nothing else!"

He spoke before the hour bell sounded, which it now did with a deep, dull, hollow, melancholy One. Light flashed up in the room upon the instant, and the curtains of his bed were drawn.

The curtains of his bed were drawn aside, I tell you, by a hand. Not the curtains at his feet, nor the curtains at his back, but those to which his face was addressed. The curtains of his bed were drawn aside; and Scrooge, starting up into a half recumbent attitude, found himself face to face with the unearthly visitor who drew them—as close to it as I am now to you, and I am standing in the spirit at your elbow.

It was a strange figure—like a child: yet not so like a child as like an old man, viewed through some supernatural medium, which gave him the appearance of having receded from the view, and being diminished to a child's proportions. Its hair, which hung about its neck and down its back, was white as if with age; and yet the face had not a wrinkle in it, and the tenderest bloom was on the skin. The arms were very long and muscular; the hands the same, as if its hold were of uncommon strength. Its legs and feet, most delicately formed, were like those upper members, bare. It wore a tunic of the purest white; and round its waist was bound a lustrous belt, the sheen of which was beautiful. It held a branch of fresh green holly in its hand; and, in singular contradiction of that wintry emblem, had its dress trimmed with summer flowers. But the strangest thing about it was, that from the crown of its head there sprung a bright clear light, by which all this was visible; and which was doubtless the occasion of its using, in its duller moments, a great extinguisher for

warned him of a visitation when the bell tolled one. He resolved to lie awake until the hour was past; and considering that he could no more go to sleep than go to Heaven, this was perhaps the wisest resolution in his power.

The quarter was so long, that he was more than once convinced he must have sunk into a doze unconsciously, and missed the clock. At length it broke upon his listening ear.

"Ding Dong!"

"A quarter past," said Scrooge, counting.

"Ding Dong!"

"Half past!" said Scrooge.

"Ding Dong!"

"A quarter to it," said Scrooge.

"Ding Dong!"

"The hour itself," said Scrooge, triumphantly, "and nothing else!"

He spoke before the hour bell sounded, which it now did with a deep, dull, hollow, melancholy ONE. Light flashed up in the room upon the instant, and the curtains of his bed were drawn.

The curtains of his bed were drawn aside, I tell you, by a hand. Not the curtains at his feet, nor the curtains at his back, but those to which his face was addressed. The curtains of his bed were drawn aside; and Scrooge, starting up into a half-recumbent attitude, found himself face to face with the unearthly visitor who drew them—as close to it as I am now to you, and I am standing in the spirit at your elbow!

It was a strange figure—like a child: yet not so like a child as like an old man viewed through some supernatural medium, which gave him the appearance of having receded from the view, and being diminished to a child's proportions. Its hair, which hung about its neck and down its back, was white as if with age; and yet the face had not a wrinkle on it, and the tenderest bloom was on the skin. The arms were very long and muscular; the hands the same; as if its hold were of uncommon strength. Its legs and feet, most delicately formed, were like those upper members, bare. It wore a tunic of the purest white; and round its waist, was bound a lustrous belt, the sheen of which was beautiful. It held a branch of fresh green holly in its hand; and, in singular contradiction of that wintry emblem, had its dress trimmed with summer flowers. But the strangest thing about it, was, that from the crown of its head there sprung a bright clear jet of light, by which all this was visible; and which was doubtless the occasion of its using, in its duller moments, a great extinguisher for a cap, which it now held under its arm.

When this Scrooge looked at it with increasing steadiness, was not its strangest quality. For as its belt sparkled and glittered now in one part and now in another, and what was light one instant at another time was dark, so the figure itself fluctuated in its distinctness: being now a thing with one arm, now with one leg, now with twenty legs, now a pair of legs without a head, now a head without a body: of which dissolving parts no outline would be visible in the dense gloom wherein they melted away. And in the very wonder of this, it would be itself again; distinct and clear as ever.

"Are you the Spirit, sir, whose coming was foretold to me?" asked Scrooge.

"I am!"

The voice was soft and gentle. Singularly low, as if instead of being so close beside him, it were at a distance.

"Who and what are you?" Scrooge demanded.

"I am the Ghost of Christmas Past."

"Long past?" inquired Scrooge: observant of its dwarfish stature.

"No. Your past."

Perhaps, Scrooge could not have told anybody why, if anybody could have asked him; but he had a special desire to see the Spirit in his cap; and begged him to be covered.

"What!" exclaimed the Ghost, "would you so soon put out, with worldly hands, the light I give? Is it not enough that you are one of those whose ruthless passions made this cap, and force me through whole trains of years to wear it low upon my brow!"

Scrooge reverently disclaimed all intention to offend, or any knowledge of having wilfully "bonneted" the Spirit at any period of his life. He then made bold to enquire what business brought him there.

"Your welfare!" said the Ghost.

Scrooge expressed himself much obliged, but could not help thinking that a night of unbroken rest would have been more conducive to that end. The Spirit must have heard him thinking, for it said immediately:

"Your reclamation then. Take heed!"

It put out its strong hand as it spoke, and clasped him gently by the arm.

"Rise! and walk with me!"

It would have been in vain for Scrooge to plead that the weather and the hour were not adapted to pedestrian purposes; that bed was warm, and the thermometer a long way below freezing; that he was clad but lightly in his slippers, think, children."

"One child," Scrooge returned.

"True," said the Ghost. "Your fellow pupil!"

Scrooge ~~said~~ and answered briefly. "Yes."

Although they had but that moment left the school behind them, they were now in the busy thoroughfares of a city, where shadowy passengers passed and repassed in one unbroken throng; where shadowy carts and coaches battled for the way, and all the noise and tumult of a real city were. It was made plain enough by the dressing of the shops, that here too it was christmas time again; but it was evening, and the streets were lighted up.

The Ghost stopped at a certain warehouse door, and asked Scrooge if he knew it.

"Know it!" said Scrooge. "Was I apprenticed here!"

They went in. At sight of an old gentleman in a Welsh wig ~~who~~ was sitting behind such a high desk, that if he had been two inches taller he must have knocked his head against the ceiling, Scrooge cried all in great excitement:

"Why, it's old Fezziwig! Bless his ~~old~~ heart: it's Fezziwig alive again!"

Old Fezziwig laid down his pen, and looked up at the clock, which pointed to the hour of seven. ~~He~~ rubbed his hands. ~~adjusted~~ his capacious waistcoat; laughed all over himself, from his shoes to his organ of benevolence; and called out in a comfortable, oily, rich fat, jovial voice:

"Yo ho, there! Ebenezer! Dick!"

Scrooge's former self, now a grown young man, came briskly in, accompanied by his fellow 'prentice.

"Dick Wilkins, to be sure!" said Scrooge. "Lord bless me yes. There he is. He was very much attached to me, was Dick. Poor Dick! Dear, dear!"

"Yo ho, my boys!" said Fezziwig. "No more work tonight! Christmas eve, Dick. Christmas, Ebenezer! Let's have the shutters up," cried old Fezziwig, with a sharp clap of his hands, "before a man can say Jack Robinson!"

You wouldn't believe how those two fellows went at it! They charged into the street with the shutters — one, two, three — had 'em up in their places — four, five, six — barred 'em and pinned 'em — seven, eight, nine — and came back before you could have got to twelve, panting like race horses.

"Hilli-ho!" cried old Fezziwig, skipping down from the high desk, with wonderful agility. "Clear away, my lads, and let's have lots of room here! Hilli-ho Dick! Chirrup, Ebenezer!"

Clear away! There was nothing they wouldn't have cleared away, or couldn't have cleared away, with old Fezziwig looking on. It was

"I have come to bring you home, dear brother!" said the child, clapping her tiny hands and bending down to laugh. "To bring you home, home, home!"

"Home, little Fan!" returned the boy.

"Yes!" said the child, brimfull of glee. "Home, for good and all. Home for ever, and ever. Father is so much kinder than he used to be, that Home's like Heaven! He spoke so gently to me one dear night when I was going to bed, that I was not afraid to ask him once more if you might come home; and he said yes you should, and sent me in a coach to bring you. And you're to be a man!" said the child, opening her eyes, "and are never to come back here; but first, we're to be together all the Christmas long, and have the merriest time in all the world."

"You are quite a woman, little Fan!" exclaimed the boy.

She clapped her hands and laughed, and tried to touch his head, but being too little, laughed again, and stood on tiptoe to embrace him. Then she began to drag him, in her childish eagerness, towards the door; and he, nothing loth to go, accompanied her.

A terrible voice in the hall cried, "Bring down Master Scrooge's box there!"; and in the hall appeared the Schoolmaster himself, who glared on Master Scrooge with a ferocious condescension, and threw him into a dreadful state of mind by shaking hands with him. He then conveyed him and his sister into the veriest old well of a shivering best parlour that ever was seen, where the maps upon the wall, and the celestial and terrestrial globes in the windows, were waxy with cold. Here he produced a decanter of curiously light wine, and a block of curiously heavy cake, and administered instalments of those dainties to the young people: at the same time, sending out a meagre servant to offer a glass of "something" to the postboy, who answered that he thanked the gentleman, but if it was the same tap as he had tasted before, he had rather not. Master Scrooge's trunk being by this time tied on to the top of the chaise, the children bade the schoolmaster good bye right willingly; and getting into it, drove gaily down the garden-sweep: the quick wheels dashing the hoar-frost and snow from off the dark leaves of the evergreens like spray.

"Always a delicate creature, whom a breath might have withered," said the Ghost. "But she had a large heart!"

"So she had," cried Scrooge. "You're right. I'll not gainsay it, Spirit. God forbid!"

"She died a woman," said the Ghost, "and had, as I

"I have come to bring you home, dear brother!" said the child, clapping her hands and bending down to laugh. "To bring you home, home, home!"

"Home, little Fan!" returned the boy.

"Yes!" said the child, brim full of glee. "Home for good and all. Home for ever and ever. Father is so much kinder than he used to be, that home's like Heaven! He spoke so gently to me one dear night when I was going to bed, that I was not afraid to ask him once more if you might come home; and he said yes you should and sent me in a coach to bring you. And you're to be a man!" said the child, opening her eyes, "and are never to come back here; but first we're to be together all the christmas long, and have the merriest time in all the world."

"You're quite a woman, little Fan!" exclaimed the boy.

She clapped her hands and laughed, and tried to touch his head; but being too little, laughed again, and stood on tiptoe to embrace him. Then she began to drag him, in her childish eagerness, towards the door; and he, nothing loth to go, accompanied her.

A terrible voice in the hall cried "Bring down master Scrooge's box there!" and in the hall appeared the schoolmaster who glared on master Scrooge with a ferocious condescension and threw him into a dreadful state by shaking hands with him. He then conveyed him and his sister into the veriest old well of a shivering best parlor that ever was seen, where the maps upon the wall, and the globes in the windows, were waxy with cold. Here he produced a decanter of curiously light wine, and a block of wonderfully heavy cake, and administered installments of those dainties to the young people: at the same time sending out a thin servant to offer a glass of "something" to the postboy, who answered that he thanked the gentleman, but if it was the same tap he had tasted before, he had rather not. Master Scrooge's trunk being by this time tied on to the top of the chaise, the children bade the schoolmaster good bye right willingly; and getting into it, drove gaily down the garden-sweep: the quick wheels dashing the hoar-frost and snow from off the dark leaves of the evergreens like spray.

"A delicate creature whom a breath might have withered," said the Ghost. "But she had a large heart!"

"So she had," cried Scrooge. "You're right. I'll not gainsay it, Spirit. God forbid!"

"She died a woman," said the Ghost "and had, as

time, just like that. Poor boy! And Valentine," said Scrooge, "and his wild brother, Orson—there they go! And what's his name who was put down in his drawers, asleep, at the Gate of Damascus—don't you see him! And the Sultan's Groom turned upside-down by the Genie—there he is upon his head! Serve him right. I'm glad of it. What business had *he* to be married to the Princess d—n him!"

To hear Scrooge expending all the earnestness of his nature on such subjects, in a most extraordinary voice between laughing and crying; and to see his heightened and excited face; would have been a surprise to his business-friends in the city, indeed!

"There's the Parrot!" cried Scrooge. "Green body and yellow tail, with a thing like a lettuce growing out of the top of his head—there he is! Poor Robin Crusoe, he called him, when he came home again after sailing round the Island. 'Poor Robin Crusoe. Where have *you* been, Robin Crusoe?' The man thought he was dreaming, but he wasn't. It was the Parrot, you know. There goes Friday—running for his life to the little creek! Halloa! Hoop! Halloa!"

Then, with a rapidity of transition very foreign to his usual character, he said, in pity for his former self, "Poor boy!" and cried again.

"I wish," Scrooge muttered, putting his hand in his pocket, and looking about him, after drying his eyes with his cuff, "but it's too late now."

"What is the matter?" asked the Spirit.

"Nothing," said Scrooge. "Nothing. There was a boy singing a Christmas Carol at my door last night. I should like to have given him something; that's all."

The Ghost smiled thoughtfully, and waved its hand: saying as it did so, "Let us see another Christmas!"

Scrooge's former self grew larger at the words, and the room became a little darker and more dirty. The panels shrunk, the windows cracked; fragments of plaster fell out of the ceiling, and the naked laths were shewn instead; but how all this was brought about, Scrooge knew no more than you do. He only knew that it was quite correct; that everything had happened so; that there he was, alone again, when all the other boys had gone home for the jolly holidays.

He was not reading now, but walking up and down despairingly. Scrooge looked at the Ghost, and with a mournful shaking of his head, glanced anxiously towards the door.

It opened; and a little girl, much younger than the boy, came darting in, and putting her arms about his neck, and often kissing him, addressed him as her "Dear dear brother."

time, just like that; and Valentine," said Scrooge, "and his wild brother, Orson - there they go! and what's his name who was put down in his drawers, asleep, at the Gate of Damascus - don't you see him! and the Sultan's Groom turned upside-down by the Genie - there he is upon his head! Serve him right. I'm glad of it. What business had he to be married to the Princess!"

To hear Scrooge expending all the earnestness of his nature on such subjects, in a most extraordinary voice between laughing and crying; and to see his heightened and excited face; would have been a surprise to his friends in the city indeed!

"There's the Parrot!" cried Scrooge. "Green body and yellow tail, with a thing like a lettuce growing out of the top of his head - there he is! Poor Robin Crusoe, he called him, when he came home again after sailing round the Island. 'Poor Robin Crusoe, where have you been, Robin Crusoe?' the man thought he was dreaming, but he wasn't. It was the Parrot, you know. There's Friday running for his life to the little creek! Halloa! Hoop! Halloa!" Then with a rapid transition very foreign to his usual character, he cried again. "Poor boy!" and cried again.

"I wish," muttered Scrooge, putting his hand in his pocket, and looking about him after drying his eyes with his cuff: "but it's too late now."

"What is the matter?" asked the Spirit.

"Nothing," said Scrooge. "Nothing. There was a boy singing a Christmas Carol at my door last night. I should like to have given him something; that's all."

The Ghost smiled thoughtfully, and waved its hand: saying as it did so, "Let us see another Christmas!"

His former self grew larger at the words, and the room became a little darker and more dirty. The panels shrunk, the windows cracked; fragments of plaster fell out of the ceiling, and the naked laths were shewn instead; but how all this was brought about, Scrooge knew no more than you do. He only knew that it was quite correct; that everything had happened so; that there he was, alone again, when all the other boys had gone home for the jolly holidays.

He was not reading now, but walking up and down despairingly. Scrooge looked at the Ghost, and with a mournful shaking of his head, glanced anxiously towards the door.

It opened: and a little girl, much younger than the boy, came darting in, and putting her arms about his neck, and often kissing him, addressed him as her "Dear, Dear brother."

leap up, as they went past! Why was he filled with gladness when he heard them give each other Merry Christmas as they parted at crossroads and bye-ways for their several homes! What was merry Christmas to Scrooge? Out upon merry Christmas. What good had it ever done to *him*?

"The School is not quite deserted," said the Ghost. "A solitary child, neglected by his friends, is left there still."

Scrooge said he knew it. And he sobbed.

They left the high road by a well-remembered lane, and soon approached a mansion of dull red brick, with a little weather-cock-surmounted cupola on the roof, and a bell hanging in it. It was a large house, but one of broken fortunes; for the spacious offices were little used, their walls were damp and mossy, their windows broken, and their gates decayed. Fowls clucked and strutted in the stables; and the coach-houses and sheds were over-run with grass. Nor was it more retentive of its ancient state, within; for entering the dreary hall, and glancing through the open doors of many rooms, they found them poorly furnished, cold, and vast. There was an earthy savour in the air, a chilly bareness in the place, which associated itself somehow with too much getting up by candle-light, and not too much to eat.

They went, the Ghost and Scrooge, across the hall, to a door at the back of the house. It opened before them, and disclosed a long bare, melancholy room, made barer still by lines of plain deal forms and desks. At one of these, a lonely boy was reading near a feeble fire; and Scrooge sat down upon a form and wept to see his poor forgotten self as he had used to be.

Not a latent echo in the house, not a squeak and scuffle from the mice behind the panelling, not a drip from the half-thawed water-spout in the dull yard behind, not a sigh among the leafless boughs of one despondent poplar, not the idle swinging of an empty store-house door, no not a clicking in the fire, but fell upon the heart of Scrooge with a softening influence, and gave a freer passage to the tears that dropped down through his fingers as he spread his hands before his face.

The Spirit touched him on the arm, and pointed to his younger self, intent upon his reading. Suddenly a man in foreign garments—wonderfully real and distinct to look at—stood outside the window, with an axe stuck in his belt, and leading an ass, laden with wood by the bridle.

"Why, it's Ali Baba!" Scrooge exclaimed in ecstasy. "It's dear old honest Ali Baba! Yes yes—I know! One Christmas time, when I—when he—when yonder solitary child was left here all alone, he *did* come, for the first past 21!

leap up, as they went ~~quite~~! ~~~~ each other Merry Christmas as they passed at cross ~~~~ and ~~~~ for their several homes! What ~~~~ Merry Christmas to Scrooge? ~~~~ out upon Merry Christmas. What good had it ever done to him?

"The school is not deserted" said the Ghost. "~~~~ a solitary child, neglected by his friends, is left ~~~~ there still."

~~Scrooge~~ said he knew it. ~~~~ ~~said~~ ~~~~, and he sobbed ~~~~

They left the ~~high road~~ by a well-remembered lane, and soon approached a ~~mansion~~ of dull red brick, with a little cupola on the roof, and a bell hanging in it. It was a large ~~~~ house, but one of broken fortunes; ~~~~ for the spacious offices were little used, their walls were damp and mossy ~~~~ their windows broken, and their gates decayed ~~~~ ~~~~ and ~~~~ in the stables; and the coach-houses and ~~~~ sheds were over-run with grass. Nor was it ~~~~ more retentive of its ancient state within; for entering the dreary hall, and glancing through the open doors of many rooms, they found them poorly furnished, cold, and vast. There was an earthy ~~~~ ~~~~ in the air, a chilly ~~~~ ~~~~ the place which associated itself somehow with too much getting up by candle-light, and not too much to eat.

They ~~~~ Scrooge, across the hall, ~~~~ to a door at the back of the house. It opened before them, and disclosed a long bare, melancholy room, made barer still by lines of plain deal forms and desks. At one ~~~~ a lonely boy was reading ~~~~ near ~~~~ a feeble fire; and Scrooge sat down upon a form and wept to see his poor forgotten self as he had used to be.

Not a latent echo in the house, not ~~~~ a drip from the water-spout in the dull yard ~~~~, not a ~~~~ ~~~~ the ~~~~ ceaseless boughs of one ~~~~ despondent poplar, not the idle swinging of an empty store-house door, no not a clicking in the fire, but fell upon the heart of Scrooge ~~~~ softening influence, and gave a freer passage to the tears ~~~~ ~~~~ ~~~~ ~~~~ course through his fingers as he spread his hands before his face! ~~~~

The Spirit touched him on the arm, and pointed to his younger self intent upon his reading. Suddenly a man ~~~~ in foreign garments ~~~~ ~~~~ the window, with an axe stuck in his belt, and leading an ass by the bridle. ~~~~

"Why, it's Ali Baba!" Scrooge exclaimed in ecstasy. "It's ~~~~ dear old honest Ali Baba! Yes, yes, I know! one Christmas time when I—when he—when ~~~~ was left here all alone, he did come, for the first

dressing-gown, and nightcap; and that he had a cold upon him at that time. The grasp though gentle as a woman's hand, was not to be resisted. He rose; but finding that the Spirit made towards the window, clasped its robe in supplication.

"I am a mortal," Scrooge remonstrated, "and liable to fall."

"Bear but a touch of my hand *there*," said the Spirit, laying it upon his heart, "and you shall be upheld in more than this!"

As the words were spoken, they passed through the wall, and stood upon an open country road, with fields on either hand. The city had entirely vanished. Not a vestige of it was to be seen. The darkness and the mist had vanished with it, for it was a clear, cold, winter day, with snow upon the ground.

"Good God!" said Scrooge, clasping his hands together as he looked about him. "I was bred in this place. I was a boy here!"

The Spirit gazed upon him mildly. Its gentle touch, though it had been light and instantaneous, appeared still present to the old man's sense of feeling. He was conscious of a thousand odours floating in the air, each one connected with a thousand thoughts, and hopes, and joys, and cares—oh! how long, long—forgotten!

"Your lip is trembling," said the Ghost. "And what is that upon your cheek?"

Scrooge muttered with an unusual catching in his voice that it was a pimple; and begged the Ghost to lead him where he would.

"You recollect the way?" inquired the Spirit.

"Remember it!" cried Scrooge with fervor. "I could walk it, blindfold."

"Strange to have forgotten it for so many years!" observed the Ghost. "Let us go on!"

They walked along the road; Scrooge recognising every gate, and post, and tree; until a little market-town appeared in the distance, with its bridge, its church and winding river. Some shaggy ponies now were seen trotting towards them with boys upon their backs, who called to other boys in country gigs and carts, driven by farmers. All these boys were in great spirits, and shouted to each other, until the broad fields were so full of merry music that the crisp air laughed to hear it.

"These are but shadows of the things that have been," said the Ghost. "They have no consciousness of us."

The jocund travellers came on; and as they came, Scrooge knew and named them every one. Why was he rejoiced beyond all bounds to see them! Why did his cold eye glisten, and his heart

think, children."

"One child," Scrooge returned.

"True," said the Ghost. "Your nephew!"

Scrooge seemed uneasy in his mind; and answered briefly, "Yes."

Although they had but that moment left the school behind them, they were now in the busy thoroughfares of a city, where shadowy passengers passed and repassed in one unbroken throng; where shadowy carts and coaches battled for the way, and all the strife and tumult of a real city were. It was made plain enough by the dressing of the shops, that here too it was Christmas time again; but it was evening, and the streets were lighted up.

The Ghost stopped at a certain warehouse door, and asked Scrooge if he knew it.

"Know it!" said Scrooge. "Was I apprenticed here!"

They went in. At sight of an old gentleman in a Welch wig, sitting behind such a high desk, that if he had been two inches taller he must have knocked his head against the ceiling, Scrooge cried in great excitement:

"Why, it's old Fezziwig! Bless his heart; it's Fezziwig alive again!"

Old Fezziwig laid down his pen, and looked up at the clock, which pointed to the hour of seven. He rubbed his hands; adjusted his capacious waistcoat; laughed all over himself, from his shoes to his organ of benevolence; and called out in a comfortable, oily, rich, fat, jovial voice:

"Yo ho, there! Ebenezer! Dick!"

Scrooge's former self, now grown a young man, came briskly in, accompanied by his fellow 'prentice.

"Dick Wilkins, to be sure!" said Scrooge to the Ghost. "Lord bless me yes. There he is. Ah! He was very much attached to me, was Dick. Poor Dick! Dear, dear!"

"Yo ho, my boys!" said Fezziwig. "No more work tonight. Christmas Eve, Dick. Christmas, Ebenezer! Let's have the shutters up," cried old Fezziwig, with a sharp clap of his hands, "before a man can say, Jack Robinson!"

You wouldn't believe how those two fellows went at it! They charged into the street with the shutters—one two three—had 'em up in their places—four five six—pinned 'em and barred 'em—seven, eight, nine—and came back before you could have got to twelve, panting like racehorses.

"Hilli-ho!" cried old Fezziwig, skipping down from the high desk, with wonderful agility. "Clear away, my lads, and let's have lots of room here! Hilli-ho, Dick! Chirrup, Ebenezer!"

Clear away! There was nothing they wouldn't have cleared away, or couldn't have cleared away, with old Fezziwig looking on. It was done in a minute. Every movable was ~~packed off~~ packed off, as if it were dismissed from public life for evermore; the floor was swept and watered, the lamps were trimmed, ~~fuel was~~ heaped up on the fire; and the warehouse was as snug and warm and dry and bright a ball-room, as you would desire to see upon a winter's night.

In came a fiddler with a music book and went up to the lofty desk, and made an orchestra ~~of it~~ and ~~tuned~~ like fifty stomach aches. In came Mrs Fezziwig, one vast substantial smile ~~as~~. In came the three Miss Fezziwigs, beaming and ~~lovable~~. In came the ~~six~~ young ~~gentlemen~~ followers whose hearts they ~~broke~~. In came all the young men and women employed in the business. In came ~~the~~ the housemaid with her cousin the baker. In came the cook with her ~~brother's particular friend~~, the milk man. In came the boy from over the way, who was suspected of ~~not~~ not having board enough from his master; trying to hide himself behind the girl from next door but one, who was proved to have had her ears pulled by her missis. In they all came one after another ~~some~~ ~~stages~~ some shyly, some boldly, some gracefully, some awkwardly, some pushing, some pulling; in they all came, anyhow and everyhow. Away they all went, twenty couple at once; hands half round and back again the other way, down the middle and up again; round and round in ~~various~~ various stages of affectionate grouping; ~~old~~ old top couple always turning up in the wrong place; new top couple starting off again as soon as ~~they got~~ they ~~got there~~; all top couples at last, and not a bottom one ~~to help them~~. When ~~this result was brought about~~, old Fezziwig ~~clapping~~ his hands ~~to stop the dance~~ cried "Well done!" and the fiddler ~~now~~ plunged his ~~hot~~ ~~red~~ face into a pot of porter, ~~especially provided for that purpose~~. But scorning rest, upon his reappearance, he instantly began again, though there were no dancers yet, as if the other fiddler had been carried home, exhausted, on a shutter; and he were a bran-new ~~fiddler~~ man resolved to ~~beat him out of sight~~ beat him out of sight, or perish.

ph 18

There were more dances, and there were forfeits, and more dances, ~~and there~~ and there was ~~negus and~~ cake, and there was negus, and there was a great piece of cold roast, and ~~there was~~ a great piece of cold ~~boiled~~ boiled, and there were mince pies and plenty of beer. But the great effect of the evening came after the roast and boiled, when the fiddler (an artful dog, ~~mind~~ the sort of man who knew his business better than ~~you or I~~ could have told it him!) struck up Sir Roger de Coverley. Then old ~~old~~ Fezziwig stood out to dance with Mrs Fezziwig. Top couple too, with a good stiff piece of work cut out for them; three or four and twenty pair of partners; people who were not to be trifled with; people who would dance, and had no notion of walking ~~straight~~.

But if they had been twice as many - ah, four times - old Fezziwig would have been a match for ~~them~~ them; and so would Mrs Fezziwig. As

done in a minute. Every moveable was packed off, as if it were dismissed from public life for evermore; the floor was swept and watered, the lamps were trimmed, fuel was heaped upon the fire; and the warehouse was as snug and warm and dry and bright a ball-room, as you would desire to see upon a winter's night.

In came a fiddler with a music book, and went up to the lofty desk, and made an orchestra of it, and tuned like fifty stomach aches. In came Mrs. Fezziwig, one vast substantial smile. In came the three Miss Fezziwigs, beaming and loveable. In came the six young followers whose hearts they broke. In came all the young men and women employed in the business. In came the housemaid with her cousin the baker. In came the cook with her brother's particular friend, the milkman. In came the boy from over the way who was suspected of not having board enough from his master; trying to hide himself behind the girl from next door but one, who was proved to have had her ears pulled by her missis. In they all came one after another, some shyly, some boldly, some gracefully, some awkwardly, some pushing, some pulling; in they all came, anyhow and everyhow. Away they all went, twenty couple at once, hands half round and back again the other way; down the middle and up again; round and round in various stages of affectionate grouping; old top couple always turning up in the wrong place; new top couple starting off again, as soon as they got there; all top couples at last, and not a bottom one to help them. When this result was brought about, old Fezziwig, clapping his hands to stop the dance, cried out "Well done!" and the fiddler plunged his hot face into a pot of porter, especially provided for that purpose. But scorning rest upon his reappearance, he instantly began again though there were no dancers yet, as if the other fiddler had been carried home, exhausted, on a shutter; and he were a bran-new man resolved to beat him out of sight, or perish.

There were more dances, and there were forfeits, and more dances and there was cake, and there was negus, and there was a great piece of cold roast, and there was a great piece of cold boiled, and there were mince pies and plenty of beer. But the great effect of the evening came after the roast and boiled, when the fiddler (an artful dog, mind! The sort of man who knew his business better than you or I could have told it him!) struck up Sir Roger de Coverley. Then old Fezziwig stood out to dance with Mrs. Fezziwig. Top couple too, with a good stiff piece of work cut out for them; three or four and twenty pair of partners; people who were not to be trifled with; people who *would* dance, and had no notion of walking.

But if they had been twice as many—ah, four times—old Fezziwig would have been a match for them, and so would Mrs. Fezziwig. As when, she was worth the his partner in every sense of the term. If that's not high praise, tell me higher, and I'll use it. A positive light appeared to issue from Fezziwig's calves. They shone in every part of the dance like moons. You couldn't have predicted at any given time what would become of 'em next. And when old Fezziwig and Mrs Fezziwig had gone all through the dance advance and retire, hold hands with your partner; bow and curtsy; corkscrew; thread the needle, and back again to your place — Fezziwig cut — cut so deftly, that he appeared to wink with his legs, and came upon his feet again without a stagger.

When the clock struck eleven, this domestic ball broke up. Mr and Mrs Fezziwig took their stations one on either side the door, and shaking hands with every person individually as he or she went out, wished him or her a merry Christmas. When everybody had retired but the two 'Prentices, they did the same by them; and thus the cheerful voices died away, and the lads were left to their beds which were under a counter in the back shop.

During the whole of this time, Scrooge had acted like a man out of his wits. His heart and soul were in the scene, and with his former self. He corroborated everything, remembered everything, enjoyed everything, and underwent the strangest agitation. It was not until now, when the bright faces of his former self and Dick were turned from them, that he remembered the Ghost, and became conscious that it was looking full upon him, while the light upon its head burnt very clear.

"A small matter," said the Ghost, "to make these silly folks so full of gratitude."

"Small!" echoed Scrooge.

The Spirit signed to him to listen to the two apprentices who were pouring out their hearts in praise of Fezziwig; and when he had done so, said. "Why! Is it not? He has spent but a few pounds of your mortal money — three or four perhaps. Is that so much that he deserves this praise?"

"It isn't that," said Scrooge, heated by the remark, and speaking unconsciously like his former — not his latter — self. "It isn't that, Spirit. He has the power to render us happy or unhappy; to make our service light or burdensome; a pleasure or a toil. Say that his power lies in words and looks; in things so slight and insignificant that it is impossible to add and count 'em up — what then? The happiness he gives is quite as great as if it cost a fortune."

He felt the Spirit's glance, and stopped.

"What is the matter?" asked the Ghost.

"Nothing particular," said Scrooge.

"Something, I think?" the Spirit insisted.

"No," said Scrooge, "No. I should like to be able to say a word or two to my clerk just now. That's all."

to *her*, she was worthy to be his partner in every sense of the term. If that's not high praise, tell me higher, and I'll use it. A positive light appeared to issue from Fezziwig's calves. They shone in every part of the dance like moons. You couldn't have predicted, at any given time, what would have become of 'em next. And when old Fezziwig and Mrs. Fezziwig had gone all through the dance—advance and retire, hold hands with your partner; bow and curtsey; corkscrew; thread the needle, and back again to your place—Fezziwig "cut"—cut so deftly, that he appeared to wink with his legs—and came upon his feet again without a stagger.

When the clock struck eleven, this domestic ball broke up. Mr. and Mrs. Fezziwig took their stations, one on either side the door, and shaking hands with every person individually as he or she went out, wished him or her a Merry Christmas. When everybody had retired but the two 'Prentices, they did the same to them; and thus the cheerful voices died away, and the lads were left to their beds: which were under a counter in the back shop.

During the whole of this time, Scrooge had acted like a man out of his wits. His heart and soul were in the scene, and with his former self. He corroborated everything, remembered everything, enjoyed everything, and underwent the strangest agitation. It was not until now, when the bright faces of his former self and Dick were turned from them, that he remembered the Ghost, and became conscious that it was looking full upon him, while the light upon its head burnt very clear.

"A small matter," said the Ghost, "to make these silly folks so full of gratitude."

"Small!" echoed Scrooge.

The Spirit signed to him to listen to the two apprentices who were pouring out their hearts in praise of Fezziwig: and when he had done so, said,

"Why! Is it not? He has spent but a few pounds of your mortal money—three or four, perhaps. Is that so much that he deserves this praise?"

"It isn't that," said Scrooge: heated by the remark and speaking unconsciously like his former—not his latter—self. "It isn't that, Spirit. He has the power to render us happy or unhappy; to make our service light or burdensome: a pleasure or a toil. Say that his power lies in words and looks; in things so slight and insignificant that it is impossible to add and count 'em up—what then? The happiness he gives, is quite as great, as if it cost a fortune."

He felt the Spirit's glance, and stopped.

"What is the matter?" asked the Ghost.

"Nothing particular," said Scrooge.

"Something, I think?" the Ghost insisted.

"No," said Scrooge, "No. I should like to be able to say a word or two to my clerk just now! That's all."

27

His former self turned down the lamps as he gave utterance to ~~these~~ the wish; and Scrooge and the Ghost again stood side by side in the open air.

"My time grows ~~very~~ short," observed the ~~last~~ Spirit. "Quick!"

This was not ~~said to~~ addressed to Scrooge, ~~or~~ or anyone whom he could see, but it produced an immediate effect. For again Scrooge ~~saw~~ himself. He was older ~~now~~ now, a man in the prime of life. His face had not the ~~harsh and~~ hard lines ~~of~~ of later years, but it had begun to wear the signs of ~~anxiety~~ care. ~~There was an eager, greedy~~ motion, restless ~~motion~~ in the eye, ~~which~~ showed ~~the passion~~ that had taken root, and where the shadow of the ~~growing~~ tree would fall.

He was not alone, but sat beside a fair young ~~girl~~ girl in a mourning dress: ~~in~~ whose eyes there were tears, ~~which~~ sparkled when ~~he~~ she sparkled in the ~~faint~~ light that shone out of the Ghost of Christmas Past.

"It matters little," she said, softly. "To you, very little. another Idol has displaced me; and if it can cheer and comfort you in time to come, as I would have ~~done~~, I have no just cause to grieve."

"What Idol has displaced you?" he ~~would do~~ rejoined.

"A golden one."

"This is the ~~even handed dealing~~ of the world!" he said. "There is nothing on which it is so hard as poverty; and there is nothing it professes to condemn ~~with such severity~~ as the pursuit of wealth!"

"You ~~fear~~ the world too much," she answered, gently. "all your other hopes ~~have merged into the hope of being~~ upon the chance of its reproach. I have seen your nobler aspirations fall off one by one, until the master passion, Gain, engrosses you. Have I not?"

"What then?" he ~~replied~~. "I have grown so much wiser, what then? I am not changed towards you."

She shook her head.

"Am I?"

"Our contract is an old one. It was made when we were both poor and content, until, in good season we could ~~better ourselves~~ improve our worldly ~~fortunes~~ by your patient industry. You are changed. When it was made, you were another man."

"I was a boy," he said impatiently.

"Your own feeling tells you that you were not what you are," she returned. "I am. That which promised happiness when we were one in heart, is ~~now~~ fraught with misery now that we are two. You often and how ~~much~~ I have thought of this, I will not say. It's enough that I have thought of it, and can release you."

"Have I ever sought release?"

His former self turned down the lamps as he gave utterance to the wish; and Scrooge and the Ghost again stood side by side, in the open air.

"My time grows short," observed the Spirit. "Quick!"

This was not addressed to Scrooge, or to any one whom he could see, but it produced an immediate effect. For again Scrooge saw himself. He was older now; a man in the prime of life. His face had not the harsh and rigid lines of later years, but it had begun to wear the signs of care and avarice. There was an eager, greedy, restless motion in the eye, which showed the passion that had taken root, and where the shadow of the growing tree would fall.

He was not alone, but sat by the side of a fair young girl in a mourning dress: in whose eyes there were tears, which sparkled in the light that shone out of the Ghost of Christmas Past.

"It matters little," she said, softly. "To you, very little. Another idol has displaced me; and if it can cheer and comfort you in time to come, as I would have tried to do, I have no just cause to grieve."

"What Idol has displaced you?" he rejoined.

"A golden one."

"This is the even-handed dealing of the world!" he said. "There is nothing on which it is so hard as poverty; and there is nothing it professes to condemn with such severity, as the pursuit of wealth!"

"You fear the world too much," she answered, gently. "All your other hopes have merged into the hope of being beyond the chance of its reproach. I have seen your nobler aspirations fall off one by one, until the master passion, Gain, engrosses you. Have I not?"

"What then?" he retorted. "Even if I have grown so much wiser, what then? I am not changed towards you."

She shook her head.

"Am I?"

"Our contract is an old one. It was made when we were both poor and content to be so, until, in good season, we could improve our worldly fortune by our patient industry. You *are* changed. When it was made, you were another man."

"I was a boy," he said impatiently.

"Your own feeling tells you that you were not what you are," she returned. "I am. That which promised happiness when we were one in heart, is fraught with misery now that we are two. How often and how keenly I have thought of this, I will not say. It is enough that I *have* thought of it, and can release you."

"Have I ever sought release!"

28

"In words - no. never."

"In what, then?"

"In a changed nature; in an altered spirit; in another atmosphere of life; another Hope as its great end. In everything that made my love of any worth or value in your sight. If this had never been between us," said the girl, looking mildly, but with steadiness, upon him; "tell me, would you seek me out and try to win me now? Ah no!"

He seemed to yield to the justice of this supposition, in spite of himself. But he said, with a struggle, "You think not."

"I would gladly think otherwise if I could," she answered. "Heaven knows! When I have learned a Truth like this, I know how strong and irresistible it must be. If you were free to-day, to-morrow, yesterday, can even I believe that you would choose a dowerless orphan girl — you, who, in your very confidence with her, weigh everything by Gain; or choosing her, if for a moment you were false enough to your one guiding principle to do so, do I not know that your repentance and regret would surely follow? I do; and I release you, with a full heart, for the love of him you once were."

He was about to speak: but with her head turned from him, she resumed.

"You may — the memory of the past half makes me hope you will — have pain in this. A very, very brief time, and you will dismiss the recollection of it gladly, as an unprofitable dream, from which it happened well that you awoke. May you be happy in the life you have chosen!"

She left him; and they parted.

"Spirit!" said Scrooge. "show me no more! Conduct me home. Why do you delight to torture me?"

"One shadow more!" exclaimed the Ghost.

"No more!" cried Scrooge. "No more. I don't wish to see it. Show me no more!" and as he spoke he pressed his hands against his head, and stamped upon the ground.

But the relentless Ghost, pinioned him in both his arms, and forced him to observe what happened next.

They were in another scene and place; a room, not very large or handsome, but full of comfort. Near to the winter fire sat a beautiful young girl, so like the last, that Scrooge believed it was the same, until he saw her, now a comely matron, sitting opposite her daughter. The noise in this room was perfectly tumultuous, for there were more children there, than Scrooge in his agitated state of mind could count.

"In words—no. Never."

"In what, then?"

"In a changed nature; in an altered spirit; in another atmosphere of life; another Hope as its great end. In everything that made my love of any worth or value in your sight. If this had never been between us," said the girl, looking mildly, but with steadiness, upon him; "tell me, would you seek me out and try to win me now? Ah, no!"

He seemed to yield to the justice of this supposition, in spite of himself. But he said, with a struggle, "You think not."

"I would gladly think otherwise if I could," she answered, "Heaven and my own soul decide! When I have learned a Truth like this, I know how strong and irresistible it must be. If you were free today, tomorrow, yesterday, can even *I* believe that you would choose a dowerless orphan girl—you, who in your very confidence with her, weigh everything by Gain: or, choosing her, if for a moment you were false enough to your one guiding principle to do so, do I not know that your repentance and regret would surely follow! I do; and I release you—with a full heart, for the love of him you once were."

He was about to speak; but with her head turned from him, she resumed.

"You may—the memory of what is past half makes me hope you will—have pain in this. A very, very brief time, and you will dismiss the recollection of it, gladly, as an unprofitable dream, from which it happened well that you awoke. May you be happy in the life you have chosen!"

She left him; and they parted.

"Spirit!" said Scrooge, "shew me no more! Conduct me home. Why do you delight to torture me?"

"One shadow more!" exclaimed the Ghost.

"No more!" cried Scrooge. "No more. I don't wish to see it. Shew me no more!"

But the relentless Ghost pinioned him in both his arms, and forced him to observe what happened next.

They were in another scene and place: a room, not very large or handsome, but full of comfort. Near to the winter fire, sat a beautiful young girl, so like the last that Scrooge believed it was the same until he saw *her*, now a comely matron, sitting opposite her daughter. The noise in this room was perfectly tumultuous, for there were more children there, than Scrooge in his agitated state of mind could

count; and unlike the celebrated herds in the poem, they were not
four conducting themselves like one; but every child was conducting
itself like forty. unanimous
no one refused to care; on the contrary the mother and daughter
laughed heartily and enjoyed it so much; and the
latter soon in the sport, her
what would I not have
given — one of them; no, no! I wouldn't for the wealth of all
the world have crushed that braided hair, and torn it down; and for
the dainty little shoe, I wouldn't have plucked it off. God bless my soul!
to wax my life, measuring her waist in
sport, this slick saucy word. I couldn't have done it —
have flown round it, and come straight again — and yet I should
have dearly liked, I own, to touch her lips; to question her that she might have opened
them; to look upon the lashes of her downcast eyes and never raise a blush; to let loose
waves of hair, I do confess, would be a
I should have liked
and yet new man enough to
him its value.

But now a knocking at the door was heard, and
that she with laughing face and
was towards it, in the presence of a
in advance of a annually maintained in that family on
attended by a When the shouting and the struggling, and
the onslaught that was made on the defenceless! The scaling him
with chairs, instead of ladders, to despoil him of brown paper parcels, hold
him by his cravat, hug him round the neck, pummel his back, and
kick his in irrepressible affection! The shouts of wonder and
delight with which the development of every package was received!
The announcement that the baby had
been in his mouth, and was more than suspected of having swallowed
a fictitious turkey on a wooden platter! The
immense relief of finding this a false alarm! The
ecstasy! They are all indescribable alike. It is enough that
the children and their emotions got out of
the parlor, and one stair at a time, up to
the top of the house; where they went to bed, and so subsided.
looked on more than ever when the master of
sat down his own fireside; and when he thought
that such another

count; and unlike the celebrated herd in the poem, they were not forty children conducting themselves like one, but every child was conducting itself like forty. The consequences were uproarious beyond belief, but no one seemed to care; on the contrary the mother and her daughter laughed heartily and enjoyed it very much; and the latter, soon beginning to mingle in the sports, got pillaged by the young brigands most ruthlessly. What would I not have given to be one of them; though I never could have been so rude, no no! I wouldn't for the wealth of all the world have crushed that braided hair and torn it down; and for the dainty little shoe, I wouldn't have plucked it off, God bless my soul! to save my life. As to measuring her waist in sport, as they did, saucy brood, I couldn't have done it—I should have expected my arm to have grown round it, for a punishment, and never come straight again—And yet—I should have dearly liked, I own, to touch her lips; to question her that she might have opened them; to look upon the lashes of her downcast eyes, and never raised a blush; to have let loose waves of hair, an inch of which would be a keepsake beyond price: in short, I should have liked, I do confess, to have had the lightest license of a child, and yet been man enough to know its value.

But now a knocking at the door was heard, and such a rush immediately ensued, that she with laughing face and plundered dress was borne towards it the centre of a flushed and boisterous group, just in time to greet the father, who in observance of a custom annually maintained in that family on Christmas Eve, came home attended by a man laden with Christmas toys and presents. Then the shouting and the struggling, and the onslaught that was made on the defenceless porter! The scaling him with chairs instead of ladders, to dive into his pockets, despoil him of brown paper parcels, hold on tight by his cravat, hug him round the neck, pommel his back, and kick his legs in irrepressible affection! The shouts of wonder and delight with which the developement of every package was received! The terrible announcement that the baby had been taken in the act of putting a doll's frying-pan into his mouth, and was more than suspected of having swallowed a fictitious turkey on a wooden platter! The immense relief of finding this a false alarm! The joy and gratitude and ecstasy! They are all indescribable alike. It is enough that by degrees the children and their emotions got out of the parlour and, by one stair at a time, up to the top of the house; where they went to bed, and so subsided.

And now Scrooge looked on more attentively than ever, when the master of the house, having his daughter leaning fondly on him, sat down with her and her mother at his own fireside; and when he thought that such another creature, quite as graceful and as full of promise, might have called him father, and been the spring-time in the winter of his life.

"Belle," said the husband, turning to his wife with a smile, "I saw an old friend of yours this afternoon."

"Who was it?"

"Guess!"

"How can I! Tut, don't I know," she added in the same breath, laughing as he laughed. "Mr Scrooge."

"Mr Scrooge it was. I passed his office window; and as it wasn't shut up, and he had a candle inside, I could scarcely help seeing him. His partner lies upon the point of death, I hear; and there he sat alone. Quite alone in the world, I do believe."

"Spirit!" said Scrooge, in a broken voice, "remove me from this place."

"I told you these were Shadows of the things that have been," said the Ghost. "That they are what they are, do not blame me!"

"Remove me!" Scrooge exclaimed. "I cannot bear it!"

He turned upon the Ghost, and seeing that it looked upon him with a face, in which in some strange way there were fragments of all the faces it had shewn him, wrestled with it.

"Leave me! Take me back. Haunt me no longer!"

In the struggle; if that can be called a struggle in which the Ghost with no visible resistance on its own part was undisturbed by any effort of its adversary, Scrooge observed that its light was burning high and bright; and dimly connecting that with its influence over him, he seized the extinguisher-cap, and by a sudden action pressed it down upon its head.

The Spirit dropped beneath it, so that the extinguisher covered its whole form; but though Scrooge pressed it down with all his force, he could not hide the light which streamed from under it, in one unbroken flood upon the ground.

He was conscious of being exhausted, and overcome by an irresistible drowsiness; and further, of being in his own bedroom. He gave the cap a parting squeeze, in which his hand relaxed; and had barely time to reel to bed, before he sunk into a heavy sleep.

creature, quite as graceful and as full of promise, might have called him father, and been a spring-time in the haggard winter of his life, his sight grew very dim indeed.

"Belle," said the husband, turning to his wife with a smile. "I saw an old friend of yours this afternoon."

"Who was it?"

"Guess!"

"How can I? Tut, don't I know," she added in the same breath, laughing as he laughed. "Mr. Scrooge."

"Mr. Scrooge it was. I passed his office window; and as it wasn't shut up, and he had a candle inside, I could scarcely help seeing him. His partner lies upon the point of Death, I hear; and there he sat alone. Quite alone in the world, I do believe."

"Spirit!" said Scrooge, in a broken voice, "remove me from this place."

"I told you these were shadows of the things that have been," said the Ghost. "That they are what they are, do not blame me!"

"Remove me!" Scrooge exclaimed. "I cannot bear it!"

He turned upon the Ghost, and seeing that it looked upon him with a face, in which, in some strange way there were fragments of all the faces it had shown him, wrestled with it.

"Leave me! Take me back. Haunt me no longer!"

In the struggle, if that can be called a struggle in which the Ghost with no visible resistance on its own part was undisturbed by any effort of its adversary; Scrooge observed that its light was burning high and bright: and dimly connecting that with its influence over him, he seized the extinguisher-cap, and by a sudden action pressed it down upon its head.

The Spirit dropped beneath it, so that the extinguisher covered its whole form; but though Scrooge pressed it down with all his force, he could not hide the light which streamed from under it, in one unbroken flood upon the ground.

He was conscious of being exhausted, and overcome by an irresistible drowsiness; and, further, of being in his own bedroom. He gave the cap a parting squeeze in which his hand relaxed; and had barely time to reel to bed, before he sank into a heavy sleep.

31

Stave III.

The Second of the Three Spirits.

Awaking in the middle of a prodigiously tough snore, and sitting up in bed to get his thoughts together, Scrooge had no occasion to be told that the Bell was again upon the stroke of One. He felt that he was restored to consciousness in the nick of time, for the especial purpose of holding a conference with the second messenger despatched to him through Jacob Marley's intervention. But finding that he turned uncomfortably cold when he began to wonder which of his curtains this new Spectre would draw back, he put them every one aside with his own hands, and lying down again, established a sharp look-out all round the bed. For he wished to challenge the Spirit on the moment of its appearance, and did not wish to be taken by surprise and made nervous.

Gentlemen of the free and easy sort, who plume themselves on being acquainted with a move, and being usually equal to the time of day, express the wide range of their capacity for adventure by observing that they are good for anything from pitch-and-toss to manslaughter; between which opposite extremes, no doubt, there lies a tolerably wide and comprehensive range of subjects. Without venturing for Scrooge quite as hardily as this, I don't mind calling on you to believe that he was ready for a good broad field of strange appearances, and that nothing between a Baby and a Rhinoceros would have astonished him very much.

Now, being prepared for almost anything, he was not by any means prepared for nothing; and consequently, when the Bell struck One, and no shape appeared, he was taken with a violent fit of trembling. Five minutes, ten minutes, a quarter of an hour went by, yet nothing came. All this time, he lay upon his bed, the very core and centre of a blaze of ruddy light, which streamed upon it when the clock proclaimed the hour; and which, being only light, was more alarming than a dozen ghosts, as he was powerless to make out what it meant, or would be at; and was sometimes apprehensive that he might be at that very moment an interesting case of spontaneous combustion, without having the consolation of knowing it.

At last, however, he began to think—as you or I would have thought at first; for it is always the person not in the predicament who knows what ought to have been done in it, and would unquestionably have done it too—at last, I say, he began to think that the source and secret of this ghostly light might be in the adjoining room; from

STAVE III.

The Second of the Three Spirits.

Awaking in the middle of a prodigiously tough snore, and sitting up in bed to get his thoughts together, Scrooge had no occasion to be told that the bell was again upon the stroke of One. He felt that he was restored to consciousness in the right nick of time, for the especial purpose of holding a conference with the second messenger despatched to him through Jacob Marley's intervention. But finding that he turned uncomfortably cold when he began to wonder which of his curtains this new Spectre would draw back, he put them every one aside with his own hands—and lying down again, established a sharp look-out all round the bed. For he wished to challenge the Spirit on the moment of its appearance, and did not wish to be taken by surprise and made nervous.

Gentlemen of the free and easy sort, who plume themselves on being acquainted with a move or two, and being usually equal to the time of day, express the wide range of their capacity for adventure, by observing that they are good for anything from pitch-and-toss to manslaughter; between which opposite extremes, no doubt there lies a tolerably wide and comprehensive range of subjects. Without venturing for Scrooge quite as hardily as this, I don't mind calling on you to believe that he was ready for a good broad field of strange appearances, and that nothing between a baby and a Rhinoceros would have astonished him very much.

Now, being prepared for almost anything, he was not by any means prepared for nothing; and, consequently, when the Bell struck One and no shape appeared, he was taken with a violent fit of trembling. Five minutes, ten minutes, a quarter of an hour went by, yet nothing came. All this time, he lay upon his bed, the very core and centre of a blaze of ruddy light which streamed upon it when the clock proclaimed the hour; and which being only light, was more alarming than a dozen ghosts, as he was powerless to make out what it meant, or would be at and was sometimes apprehensive that he might be at that very moment an interesting case of spontaneous combustion, without having the consolation of knowing it.

At last, however, he began to think—as you or I would have thought at first; for it is always the person *not* in the predicament who knows what ought to have been done in it, and would unquestionably have done it too—at last, I say, he began to think that the source and secret of this ghostly light might be in the adjoining room: from on further knuckling it, it seemed to hiss. The

whence it issued. This idea taking full possession of
his mind he got up softly, and shuffled in his slippers
to the door. At the light that shone upon the lock

the moment Scrooge's hand was upon the lock a strange voice called
him by his name, and bade him enter. He obeyed. thrusting in his
head.

It was his own room. There was no doubt about that. But it had
undergone a surprising transformation. The walls and ceiling were so
hung with living green, that it looked a perfect grove, from
every part of which the bright gleaming berries glistened. The crisp
leaves of the holly, mistletoe, and ivy, reflected the light bright as if
so many little mirrors had been scattered there; and such a mighty blaze
went roaring up the chimney, as that dull hearth had never
known in Scrooge's time, or Marley's, or for many and many a Winter Season
Heaped up upon the floor were turkeys, geese, game, poultry,
joints of meat, mince-pies, plum-puddings, barrels of oysters, red hot chestnuts,
cherry-cheeked apples, juicy oranges, luscious pears, immense
twelfth-cakes, and seething bowls of Punch.
Upon this couch, there sat a jolly Giant, glorious to see,
who bore a glowing torch, in shape not unlike Plenty's horn, and held it up
high up, Scrooge, as he came peeping
round the door.

"Come in!" exclaimed the Ghost. "Come in! and know me better
man!"

Scrooge entered timidly, and hung his head before this Spirit. He was not the
dogged Scrooge he had been; and though the Spirit's eyes were clear and kind, he did not like to
meet them. "I am the Ghost of Christmas Present," said the Spirit. "Look upon
me!"

Scrooge reverently did so. It was clothed in one simple deep green mantle,
bordered with white fur. This garment hung so loosely on the figure, that its
capacious breast was bare, as if disdaining to be warded or concealed
by any artifice. Its feet, observable beneath the ample folds of the garment,
were also bare; and on its head it wore no other covering than a holly
wreath, set here and there with shining icicles. Its
genial face, its sparkling eye, its open hand, its cheery voice, its unconstrained
demeanour, and its joyful air. Girded round its middle
was an antique scabbard; but no sword was in it, and the ancient
sheath was eaten up with rust.

"You have never seen the like of me before!" exclaimed

whence, on further tracing it, it seemed to shine. This idea taking full possession of his mind, he got up softly, and shuffled in his slippers to the door.

The moment Scrooge's hand was on the lock, a strange voice called him by his name, and bade him enter. He obeyed, thrusting in his head.

It was his own room. There was no doubt about that. But it had undergone a surprising transformation. The walls and ceiling were so hung with living green, that it looked a perfect grove, from every part of which bright gleaming berries glistened. The crisp leaves of holly, mistletoe, and ivy, reflected back the light, as if so many little mirrors had been scattered there; and such a mighty blaze went roaring up the chimney as that dull petrification of a hearth had never known in Scrooge's time, or Marley's, or for many and many a winter season gone. Heaped up upon the floor, to form a kind of throne, were turkeys, geese, game, poultry, brawn, great joints of meat, suckling pigs, long wreaths of sausages, mince-pies, plum puddings, barrels of oysters, red hot chestnuts, cherry-cheeked apples, juicy oranges, luscious pears, immense twelfth cakes, and seething bowls of Punch, that made the chamber dim with their delicious steam. In easy state upon this couch, there sat a jolly Giant, glorious to see, who bore a glowing torch, in shape not unlike Plenty's horn, and held it up, high up, to shed its light on Scrooge, as he came peeping round the door.

"Come in!" exclaimed the Ghost. "Come in! and know me better man!"

Scrooge entered timidly, and hung his head before this Spirit. He was not the dogged Scrooge he had been; and though its eyes were clear and kind, he did not like to meet them.

"I am the Ghost of Christmas Present," said the Spirit. "Look upon me!"

Scrooge reverently did so. It was clothed in one simple, deep green robe or mantle bordered with white fur. This garment hung so loosely on the figure, that its capacious breast was bare, as if disdaining to be warded or concealed by any artifice. Its feet, observable beneath the ample folds of the garment, were also bare: and on its head it wore no other covering than a holly wreath set here and there, with shining icicles. Its dark brown curls were long and free: free as its genial face, its sparkling eye, its open hand, its cheery voice, its unconstrained demeanour, and its joyful air. Girded round its middle was an antique scabbard; but no sword was in it, and the ancient sheath was eaten up with rust.

"You have never seen the like of me before!" exclaimed

the Spirit.

"Never", Scrooge made answer to it.

"Have never walked forth with the younger members of my family; meaning (for I am very young) my elder brothers born in these later years?" pursued the Phantom.

"I don't think I have", said Scrooge. "I am afraid I have not. Have you many brothers, Spirit?"

"More than Eighteen hundred", said the Ghost.

"A tremendous family to provide for!" muttered Scrooge.

The Ghost of Christmas Present rose, and as it did, so Scrooge observed that its skirts seemed to have some object which it sought to hide. He fancied that he saw a foot, much smaller than the Spirit, protruding for a moment from its robe; and being curious in everything concerning these unearthly visitors, he asked the Spirit what it meant.

"They are not so many as they might be", replied the Ghost, "who care to know or ask. No matter what it is, just now, are you ready to go forth with me?"

"Spirit!" said Scrooge, submissively, "conduct me where you will. I went last night on compulsion, and I learnt a lesson which is working now. Tonight, if you have aught to teach me, let me profit by it."

"Touch my robe!"

Scrooge did as he was told, and held it fast.

Holly, mistletoe, red berries, ivy, turkeys, geese, game, poultry, brawn, meat, pigs, sausages, oysters, pies, puddings, fruit and punch, all vanished instantly. So did the room, the fire, the ruddy glow, the hour of night; and they stood in the city streets on christmas morning, where (for the weather was severe) the people made a rough but not unpleasant kind of music, in scraping the snow from the pavement in front of their dwellings, and from the tops of their houses, whence it was mad delight to the boys to see it come plumping down into the road below, and splitting into artificial little snow-storms.

The house fronts looked black enough, and the windows blacker, contrasting in the white sheet of snow upon the roofs, and in the dirtier snow upon the ground; which last was deposit had been ploughed up in deep furrows by the heavy wheels of carts and waggons — furrows that crossed and recrossed each other hundreds of times where the great streets branched off; and made intricate channels, hard to trace, in the thick yellow mud and

the Spirit.

"Never," Scrooge made answer to it.

"Have never walked forth with the younger members of my family; meaning (for I am very young) my elder brothers born in these later years!" pursued the Phantom.

"I don't think I have," said Scrooge. "I am afraid I have not. Have you had many brothers, Spirit?"

"More than eighteen hundred," said the Ghost.

"A tremendous family to provide for!" muttered Scrooge.

The Ghost of Christmas Present rose, and as it did so Scrooge observed that at its skirts it seemed to have some object which it sought to hide. He fancied that he saw either the claw of a great bird or a foot much smaller than the Spirit's own, protruding for a moment from its robes; and being curious in everything concerning these unearthly visitors, he asked the Spirit what it meant.

"They are not so many as they might be," replied the Ghost, "who care to know or ask. No matter what it is, just now. Are you ready to go forth with me?"

"Spirit," said Scrooge submissively, "conduct me where you will. I went forth last night on compulsion, and I learnt a lesson which is working now. Tonight, if you have aught to teach me, let me profit by it."

"Touch my robe!"

Scrooge did as he was told, and held it fast.

Holly, mistletoe, red berries, ivy, turkeys, geese, game, poultry, brawn, meat, pigs, sausages, oysters, pies, puddings, fruit and punch all vanished instantly. So did the room, the fire, the ruddy glow, the hour of night; and they stood in the city streets on Christmas morning, where (for the weather was severe) the people made a rough but brisk and not unpleasant kind of music, in scraping the snow from the pavement in front of their dwellings, and from the tops of their houses; whence it was mad delight to the boys to see it come plumping down into the road below, and splitting into artificial little snow-storms.

The house fronts looked black enough, and the windows blacker, contrasting with the smooth white sheet of snow upon the roofs, and with the dirtier snow upon the ground; which last deposit had been ploughed up in deep furrows by the heavy wheels of carts and waggons—furrows that crossed and recrossed each other hundreds of times where great thoroughfares branched off, and made intricate channels, hard to trace in the thick yellow mud and

icy water. The sky was gloomy, and the shortest streets were choked up
with a dingy mist half thawed half frozen, whose heavier particles descended
in a shower of sooty atoms, as if all the chimneys in Great Britain
had by one consent caught fire, and were blazing away to their dear
hearts' content. There was nothing very cheerful in the climate
or the town; yet there was an air of cheerfulness abroad, that
the clearest summer air and brightest summer sun, might have endeavoured
to diffuse, in vain.

For the people who were shovelling away on the housetops were jovial
and full: calling out to one another from the parapets, and
now and then exchanging a facetious snowball - better-natured
missile far, than many a wordy jest - laughing heartily if it went right, and not less heartily if
it went wrong. The poulterers' shops were still half open; and the
fruiterers' were radiant in their glory. There were
great, round, pot-bellied baskets of chestnuts, shaped like the waistcoats of
jolly old gentlemen, lolling at the doors, and tumbling out into the street in
their apoplectic opulence. There were ruddy, brown-faced, broad-girthed Spanish
onions, shining in the fatness of their growth like Spanish friars, and
winking from their shelves in wanton slyness at the girls as they went
by. There were pears and apples, clustered high in blooming
pyramids; there were bunches of grapes, made, in the shopkeeper's benevolence, to dangle from conspicuous hooks, that people's mouths
might water gratis as they passed; there were piles of filberts, mossy and
brown, recalling, in their fragrance, ancient walks among the woods, and pleasant shufflings
ankle deep through withered leaves; there were Norfolk Biffins, squab and swarthy,
setting off the yellow of the oranges and lemons, and, in the great compactness
of their juicy persons, urgently entreating and beseeching to be carried home in
paper bags and eaten after dinner. The very gold and silver fish, set forth
among these choice fruits in a bowl, though members of a dull and stagnant-blooded race,
appeared to know that there was something going on; and, to a fish,
went gasping round
and round their little world in slow and passionless excitement.

The Grocers'! oh, the Grocers'! nearly closed, with perhaps
two shutters down, or one; but through those gaps, such glimpses!
It was not alone that the scales descending on the
counter made a merry sound, or that the twine and roller parted company so briskly,
or that the canisters were rattled up and down like juggling tricks, or even that the blended scents of tea and coffee were so grateful to the nose, or even that the raisins
were so plentiful and rare, the almonds so extremely white, the sticks
of cinnamon so long and straight, the other spices so delicious, the candied fruits so caked and spotted with molten
sugar as to make the coldest lookers-on feel faint and subse-
quently bilious. Nor was it that the figs were moist and

icy water. The sky was gloomy, and the shortest streets were choked up with a dingy mist, half thawed half frozen, whose heavier particles descended in a shower of sooty atoms as if all the chimneys in Great Britain had by one consent caught fire, and were blazing away to their dear hearts' content. There was nothing very cheerful in the climate or the town; and yet was there an air of cheerfulness abroad, that the clearest summer air and brightest summer sun, might have endeavoured to diffuse, in vain.

For the people who were shovelling away on the housetops were jovial and full of glee: calling out to one another from the parapets and now and then exchanging a facetious snowball—better-natured missile far, than many a wordy jest—laughing heartily if it went right, and not less heartily if it went wrong. The poulterer's shops were still half open; and the fruiterers were radiant in their glory. There were great, round, pot-bellied baskets of chestnuts, shaped like the waistcoats of jolly old gentlemen, lolling at the doors, and tumbling out into the street in their apoplectic opulence. There were ruddy, brown-faced, broad-girthed Spanish Onions shining in the fatness of their growth like Spanish Friars, and winking from their shelves in wanton slyness at the girls as they went by, and glanced demurely at the hung-up mistletoe. There were pears and apples clustered high in blooming pyramids; there were bunches of grapes, made, in the shopkeepers' benevolence, to dangle from conspicuous hooks, that people's mouths might water, gratis, as they passed; there were piles of filberts, mossy and brown; recalling, in their fragrance ancient walks among the woods, and pleasant shuffling, ankle deep, through withered leaves; there were Norfolk Biffins, squab and swarthy, setting off the yellow of the oranges and lemons, and in the great compactness of their juicy persons, urgently entreating and beseeching to be carried home in paper bags and eaten after dinner. The very gold and silver fish, set forth among these dainties in a bowl, though members of a dull and stagnant-blooded race appeared to know that there was something going on, and, to a fish, went gasping round and round their little world in slow and passionless excitement.

The Grocers', Oh, the Grocers!—nearly closed, with perhaps two shutters down, or one, but through those gaps, such glimpses! It was not alone that the scales descending on the counter made a merry sound or that the twine and roller parted company so briskly, or that the canisters were rattled up and down like juggling tricks, or even that the blended scents of tea and coffee were so grateful to the nose, or even that the raisins were so plentiful and rare, the almonds so extremely white, the sticks of cinnamon so long and straight, the other spices so delicious, the candied fruits so caked and spotted with molten sugar as to make the coldest lookers-on feel faint and subsequently bilious. Nor was it that the figs were moist and jolly, or the peach plums blushed in modest tartness from their highly-decorated boxes, or that everything was good to eat and in its christmas dress; but the customers were all so hurried and so eager in the hopeful promise of the day, that they tumbled up against each other at the door, crashing their wicker baskets wildly, and left their purchases upon the counter, and came running back to fetch them, and committed hundreds of the like mistakes in the best humour possible: while the grocer and his people were so frank and fresh, that the polished hearts with which they fastened their aprons behind might have been their own: worn outside for general inspection and for christmas daws to peck at if they chose.

But soon the steeples called good people all, to church and chapel, and away they came, flocking through the streets in their best clothes, and with their gayest faces. And at the same time there emerged from scores of bye-streets, lanes, and nameless turnings, innumerable people, carrying their dinners to the bakers' shops. The sight of these poor revellers appeared to interest the Spirit very much, for he stood with Scrooge beside him in a baker's doorway, and taking off the covers as their bearers passed, sprinkled incense upon their dinners from his torch. And it was a very uncommon kind of torch, for once or twice when there were angry words between some dinner-carriers who had jostled each other, he shed a few drops of water on them from it, and their good humour was restored directly. For they said, it was a shame to quarrel upon Christmas Day. And so it was! God love it, so it was!

In time the bells ceased, and the bakers were shut up. And yet there was a genial shadowing forth of all these dinners and the progress of their cooking, in the thawed blotch of wet above each baker's oven; where the pavement smoked as if its stones were cooking too.

"Is there a peculiar flavour in what you sprinkle from your torch?" asked Scrooge.

"There is. My own."

"Would it apply to any kind of dinner on this day?" asked Scrooge.

"To any kindly given. To a poor one most."

"Why to a poor one most?" asked Scrooge.

"Because it needs it most."

"Spirit," said Scrooge, after a moment's thought, "I wonder you, of all the beings in the many worlds about us, should desire to cramp these people's opportunities of innocent enjoyment."

"I!" cried the Spirit, proudly.

"Why, you would deprive them of their means of dining every seventh day, often the only day on which they can be said to dine at all," said Scrooge. "Wouldn't you?"

"I!" cried the Spirit.

pulpy, or that the French plums blushed in modest tartness from their highly decorated boxes, or that everything was good to eat and in its Christmas dress: but the customers were all so hurried and so eager in the hopeful promise of the Day, that they tumbled up against each other at the door, clashing their wicker baskets wildly; and left their purchases upon the counter, and came running back to fetch them, and committed hundreds of the like mistakes in the best humour possible: while the Grocer and his people were so frank and fresh, that the polished hearts with which they fastened their aprons behind, might have been their own: worn outside for general inspection and for Christmas Daws to peck at if they chose.

But soon the steeples called good people all, to church and chapel, and away they came, flocking through the streets in their best clothes, and with their gayest faces. And at the same time there emerged from scores of bye streets, lanes, and nameless turnings, innumerable people, carrying their dinners to the bakers' shops. The sight of these poor revellers appeared to interest the Spirit very much, for he stood with Scrooge beside him in a baker's doorway, and taking off the covers as their bearers passed sprinkled fire upon their dinners from his torch. And it was a very uncommon kind of Torch, for once or twice when there were angry words between some dinner-carriers who had jostled with each other, he shed a few drops of water on them from it, and their good humour was restored directly. For they said, it was a shame to quarrel upon Christmas Day. And so it was! God love it, so it was!

In time the bells ceased, and the bakers' were shut up; and yet there was a genial shadowing forth of all these dinners and the progress of their cooking, in the thawed blotch of wet above each bakers' oven: where the pavement smoked, as if its stones were cooking too.

"Is there a peculiar flavor in the fire you sprinkle from your Torch?" asked Scrooge.

"There is. My own."

"Would it apply to any kind of dinner on this day?" asked Scrooge.

"To any kindly given. To a poor one most."

"Why to a poor one most?" asked Scrooge.

"Because it needs it most."

"Spirit," said Scrooge, after a moment's thought; "I wonder you, of all the Beings in the many Worlds about us, should desire to cramp these people's opportunities of innocent enjoyment."

"*I!*" cried the Spirit, proudly.

"Why, you would deprive them of their means of dining every seventh day—often the only day on which they can be said to dine at all." said Scrooge. "Wouldn't you?"

"*I!*" cried the Spirit.

"Would you close these places on the Seventh Day?" said Scrooge.

"I seek!" explained the Spirit.

"It has been done in your name, or at least in that of your family," said Scrooge.

"There are some upon this earth of yours," returned the Spirit, "who lay claim to know us, and who do their deeds of passion, pride, ill-will, hatred, envy, bigotry, and selfishness in our name, who are as strange to us and all our kith and kin, as if they had never lived. Remember that, and charge their doings on themselves; not us."

Scrooge promised that he would; and they went on, invisible, as they had been before, into the suburbs of the town. It was a remarkable property of the Ghost (which Scrooge had observed at the baker's) that notwithstanding his gigantic size, he could accommodate himself to any place with ease; and that he stood beneath a low roof quite as gracefully, and like a supernatural creature, as it was possible he could have done in any lofty hall.

And perhaps it was the pleasure the good Spirit had in showing off this power of his, or else it was his own kind, generous, hearty nature, and his sympathy with all poor men, that led him straight to Scrooge's clerk's; for there he went, and took Scrooge with him, holding to his robe; and on the threshold of the door the Spirit smiled, and stopped to bless Bob Cratchit's dwelling with the sprinkling of his torch. Think of that! Bob had but fifteen "Bob" a-week himself; he pocketed on Saturdays but fifteen copies of his Christian name; and yet the Ghost of Christmas Present blessed his four-roomed house!

Then up rose Mrs Cratchit, Cratchit's wife, dressed out but poorly in a twice-turned gown, but brave in ribbons, which are cheap and make a goodly show for sixpence; and she laid the cloth, assisted by Belinda Cratchit, second of her daughters, also brave in ribbons; while Master Peter Cratchit plunged a fork into the saucepan of potatoes, and getting the corners of his monstrous shirt-collar (Bob's private property, conferred upon his son and heir in honour of the day) into his mouth, rejoiced to find himself so gallantly attired, and yearned to show his linen in the fashionable Parks. And now two smaller Cratchits, boy and girl, came tearing in, screaming that outside the baker's they had smelt the goose, and known it for their own; and basking in luxurious thoughts of sage and onion, these young Cratchits danced about the table, and exalted Master Peter Cratchit to the skies, while he (not proud, although his collars nearly choked him) blew the fire, until the slow potatoes bubbling up, knocked loudly at the saucepan-lid to be let out and peeled.

"What has ever got your precious father then?" said Mrs Cratchit. "And your brother, Tiny Tim! And Martha warn't as late last Christmas Day by half-an-hour!" "Here's Martha, mother!" said a girl, appearing as she spoke.

"You seek to close these places on the Seventh Day?" said Scrooge. "And it comes to the same thing."

"*I* seek!" exclaimed the Spirit.

"Forgive me if I am wrong. It has been done in your name, or at least in that of your Family," said Scrooge.

"There are some upon this Earth of yours," returned the Spirit, "who lay claim to know us, and who do their deeds of passion, pride, ill will, hatred, envy, bigotry, and selfishness in our name; who are as strange to us and all our kith and kin, as if they had never lived. Remember that, and charge their doings on themselves; not us."

Scrooge promised that he would; and they went on, invisible as they had been before, into the suburbs of the town. It was a remarkable property of the Ghost (which Scrooge had observed at the baker's) that notwithstanding his gigantic size, he could accommodate himself to any place with ease; and that he stood beneath a low roof quite as gracefully and like a supernatural creature, as it was possible he could have done in any lofty hall.

And perhaps it was the pleasure the good Spirit had in shewing off this power of his, or else it was his own kind, generous, hearty nature, and his sympathy with all poor men that led him straight to Scrooge's clerk's; for there he went, and took Scrooge with him holding to his robe; and on the threshold of the door the Spirit smiled, and stopped to bless Bob Cratchit's dwelling with the sprinkling of his torch. Think of that! Bob had but fifteen "Bob" a week himself—he pocketed on Saturdays but fifteen copies of his Christian name; and yet the Ghost of Christmas Present blessed his four-roomed house.

Then up rose Mrs. Cratchit, Cratchit's wife, dressed out but poorly in a twice-turned gown, but brave in ribbons which are cheap and make a goodly show for sixpence; and she laid the cloth assisted by Belinda Cratchit, second of her daughters; also brave in ribbons; while Master Peter Cratchit plunged a fork into the saucepan of potatoes, and getting the corners of his monstrous shirt-collar (Bob's private property, conferred upon his son and heir in honor of the day) into his mouth rejoiced to find himself gallantly attired, and yearned to show his linen in the fashionable parks. And now two smaller Cratchits, boy and girl, came tearing in, screaming that outside the baker's they had smelt the goose, and known it for their own; and basking in luxurious thoughts of sage and onion, these young Cratchits danced about the table, and exalted Master Peter Cratchit to the skies, while he (not proud, although his collars nearly choked him) blew the fire, until the slow potatoes bubbling up, knocked loudly at the saucepan-lid to be let out and peeled.

"What has ever got your precious father then," said Mrs. Cratchit. "And your brother, Tiny Tim; and Martha warn't as late last Christmas Day by half an hour!"

"Here's Martha, mother!" said a girl, appearing as she spoke.

"Here's Martha, mother!" cried the two young Cratchits. "Hurrah! There's such a goose, Martha!"

"Why, bless your heart alive, my dear, how late you are!" said Mrs Cratchit, kissing her a dozen times, and taking off her shawl and bonnet for her with officious zeal.

"We'd a deal of work to finish up last night," replied the girl, "and had to clear away this morning, mother!"

"Well! Never mind so long as you are come," said Mrs Cratchit. "Sit ye down before the fire, my dear, and have a warm, Lord bless ye!"

"No, no! There's father coming," cried the two young Cratchits, who were everywhere at once. "Hide, Martha, hide!"

So Martha hid herself, and in came little Bob, the father, with at least three feet of comforter exclusive of the fringe, hanging down before him; and his threadbare clothes darned up and brushed, to look seasonable; and Tiny Tim upon his shoulder. Alas for Tiny Tim, he bore a little crutch, and had his limbs supported by an iron frame!

"Why, where's our Martha?" cried Bob Cratchit looking round.

"Not coming," said Mrs Cratchit.

"Not coming!" said Bob, with a sudden declension in his high spirits; for he had been Tim's blood horse all the way from church, and had come home rampant. "Not coming upon Christmas Day!"

Martha didn't like to see him disappointed, if it were only in joke; so she came out prematurely from behind the closet door, and ran into his arms, while the two young Cratchits hustled Tiny Tim, and bore him off into the wash-house, that he might hear the pudding singing in the copper.

"And how did little Tim behave?" asked Mrs Cratchit, when she had rallied Bob on his credulity, and Bob had hugged his daughter to his heart's content.

"As good as gold," said Bob, "and better. Somehow he gets thoughtful, sitting by himself so much, and thinks the strangest things you ever heard. He told me, coming home, that he hoped the people saw him in the church, because he was a cripple, and it might be pleasant to them to remember upon Christmas Day, who made lame beggars walk and blind men see." Bob's voice was tremulous when he told them this, and trembled more when he said that Tiny Tim was growing strong and hearty.

"Do that and Spirit?" Scrooge demanded, with an interest he had never felt before. "I see a vacant seat," replied the Ghost, "beside the chimney corner, and the child will die."

His active little crutch was heard upon the floor, and back came Tiny Tim before another word was spoken, escorted by his brother and sister to his stool before the fire; and while Bob, turning up his cuffs — as if, poor fellow, they were capable of being made more shabby — compounded some hot mixture in a jug with gin and lemons, and stirred it round and round and put it on the hob to simmer; Master Peter, and the two ubiquitous young Cratchits went to fetch the goose, with which they soon returned in high procession.

"Here's Martha mother!" cried the two young Cratchits. "Hurrah! There's *such* a goose, Martha!"

"Why, bless your heart alive my dear, how late you are!" said Mrs. Cratchit, kissing her a dozen times, and taking off her shawl and bonnet for her, with officious zeal.

"We'd a deal of work to finish up last night," replied the girl, "and had to clear away this morning, mother!"

"Well! Never mind so long as you are come," said Mrs. Cratchit. "Sit ye down before the fire, my dear, and have a warm, Lord bless ye!"

"No no! There's father coming," cried the two young Cratchits who were everywhere at once. "Hide, Martha, hide!"

So Martha hid herself, and in came little Bob, the father, with at least three feet of comforter exclusive of the fringe, hanging down before him; and his thread-bare clothes darned up and brushed, to look seasonable; and Tiny Tim upon his shoulder. Alas for Tiny Tim, he bore a little crutch; and had his limbs supported by an iron frame!

"Why, where's our Martha!" cried Bob Cratchit looking round.

"Not coming," said Mrs. Cratchit.

"Not coming!" said Bob, with a sudden declension in his high spirits—for he had been Tim's blood horse all the way from church, and had come home rampant. "Not coming upon Christmas Day!"

Martha didn't like to see him disappointed, if it were only in joke; so she came out prematurely from behind the closet door, and ran into his arms, while the two young Cratchits hustled Tiny Tim, and bore him off into the wash-house, that he might hear the pudding singing in the copper.

"And how did little Tim behave?" asked Mrs. Cratchit, when she had rallied Bob on his credulity, and Bob had hugged his daughter to his heart's content.

"As good as gold," said Bob, "and better. Somehow he gets thoughtful sitting by himself so much, and thinks the strangest things you ever heard. He told me, coming home that he hoped the people saw him in the church because he was a cripple, and it might be pleasant to them to remember upon Christmas Day who made lame beggars walk and blind men see."

Bob's voice was tremulous when he told them this, and trembled more when he said that Tiny Tim was growing strong and hearty.

His active little crutch was heard upon the floor, and back came Tiny Tim before another word was spoken, escorted by his brother and sister to his stool before the fire; and while Bob turning up his cuffs—as if, poor fellow, they were capable of being made more shabby!—compounded some hot mixture in a jug with gin and lemons, and stirred it round and round and put it on the hob to simmer, Master Peter and the two ubiquitous young Cratchits went to fetch the goose, with which they soon returned in High Procession.

Such a bustle ensued that you might have thought a goose the rarest of all birds; a feathered phenomenon with a black swan was a matter of course — and in truth it was something very like it in that house. Mrs Cratchit made the gravy (ready beforehand in a little saucepan) hissing hot; Master Peter mashed the potatoes with incredible vigour. Miss Belinda sweetened up the apple sauce; Martha dusted the hot plates; Bob took Tiny Tim beside him in a tiny corner at the table; the two young Cratchits set chairs for everybody, not forgetting themselves, and mounting guard upon their posts, crammed spoons into their mouths, lest they should shriek for goose before their turn came to be helped. At last the dishes were set on, and grace was said. It was succeeded by a breathless pause, as Mrs Cratchit, looking slowly all along the carving knife, prepared to plunge it into the breast; but when she did, and when the long-expected gush of stuffing issued forth, one murmur of delight arose all round the table, and even Tiny Tim, excited by the two young Cratchits, beat on the table with the handle of his knife and cried Hurrah!

There never was such a goose. Bob said he didn't believe there ever was such a goose cooked. Its tenderness and flavor, size and cheapness, were the themes of universal admiration. Eked out by the apple sauce and mashed potatoes, it was a sufficient dinner for the whole family; indeed, as Mrs Cratchit said with great delight, they hadn't ate it all at last! Yet every one had had enough, and the youngest Cratchits in particular were steeped in sage and onion to the eyebrows. But now the plates being changed by Miss Belinda, Mrs Cratchit left the room alone — too nervous to bear witnesses — to take the pudding up, and bring it in.

Suppose it should not be done enough! Suppose it should break in turning out! Suppose somebody should have got over the wall of the back yard, and stolen it, while they were merry with the goose — a supposition at which the two young Cratchits became livid! All sorts of horrors were supposed.

Hallo! A great deal of steam! The pudding was out of the copper. A smell like a washing-day! That was the cloth. A smell like an eating-house and a pastry cook's next door to each other, with a laundress's next door to that! That was the pudding. In half a minute Mrs Cratchit entered — flushed, but smiling proudly — with the pudding, like a speckled cannon ball, so hard and firm, blazing in half of half a quartern of ignited brandy, and bedight with Christmas holly stuck into the top!

Oh a wonderful pudding! Bob Cratchit said, and calmly too, that he regarded it as the greatest success achieved by Mrs Cratchit since their marriage. Mrs Cratchit said that now the weight was off her mind, she would confess she

Such a bustle ensued that you might have thought a goose the rarest of all birds; a feathered phenomenon, to which a black swan was a matter of course— and in truth it was something very like it in that house. Mrs. Cratchit made the gravy (ready beforehand in a little saucepan) hissing hot; Master Peter mashed the potatoes with incredible vigour; Miss Belinda sweetened up the apple sauce; Martha dusted the hot plates; Bob took Tiny Tim beside him in a tiny corner at the table; the two young Cratchits set chairs for everybody, not forgetting themselves, and mounting guard upon their posts, crammed spoons into their mouths, lest they should shriek for goose before their turn came to be helped. At last the dishes were set on, and grace was said. It was succeeded by a breathless pause as Mrs. Cratchit looking slowly all along the carving knife, prepared to plunge it in the breast; but when she did, and when the long-expected gush of stuffing issued forth, one murmur of delight arose all round the board, and even Tiny Tim, excited by the two young Cratchits, beat on the table with the handle of his knife, and feebly cried Hurrah!

There never was such a goose. Bob said he didn't believe there ever was such a goose cooked. Its tenderness and flavor, size and cheapness, were the themes of universal admiration. Eked out by the apple sauce and mashed potatoes it was a sufficient dinner for the whole family; indeed, as Mrs. Cratchit said with great delight (surveying one small atom of a bone upon the dish) they hadn't ate it all at last! Yet every one had had enough, and the youngest Cratchits in particular were steeped in sage and onion to the eyebrows! But now the plates being changed by Miss Belinda, Mrs. Cratchit left the room alone—too nervous to bear witnesses— to take the pudding up, and bring it in.

Suppose it should not be done enough! Suppose it should break in turning out! Suppose somebody should have got over the wall of the back-yard, and stolen it, while they were merry with the goose—a supposition at which the two young Cratchits became livid! All sorts of horrors were supposed.

Hallo! A great deal of steam! The pudding was out of the copper. A smell like a washing-day! That was the cloth. A smell like an eating house, and a pastry cook's next door to each other, with a laundress's next door to that! That was the pudding. In half a minute Mrs. Cratchit entered—flushed, but smiling proudly— with the pudding, like a speckled cannon ball, so hard and firm, blazing in half of half a quartern of ignited brandy, and bedight with Christmas Holly stuck into the top!

Oh a wonderful pudding! Bob Cratchit said, and calmly too, that he regarded it as the greatest success achieved by Mrs. Cratchit since their marriage. Mrs. Cratchit said that now the weight was off her mind, she would confess she and had her doubts about the quantity of flour. But everybody had something to say about it, but nobody said or thought it was at all a small pudding for a large family. It would have been flat heresy to do so. Any Cratchit would have blushed to hint at such a thing.

At last the dinner was all done; and the cloth was cleared and the hearth swept, and the fire made up. The compound in the jug being tasted and considered perfect, apples and oranges were put upon the table, and a shovel full of chestnuts on the fire. Then all the family drew round the hearth, in what Bob Cratchit called a circle — meaning half a one — and at Bob Cratchit's elbow stood the family display of glass: two tumblers, and a custard cup without a handle.

These held the hot stuff from the jug, however, as well as golden goblets would have done; and Bob served it out with beaming looks, while the chestnuts on the fire sputtered and cracked noisily. Then Bob proposed:

"A merry Christmas to us all my dears. God bless us!"

Which all the family re-echoed.

"God bless us every one!" said Tiny Tim, the last of all.

He sat very close to his father's side upon his little stool. Bob held his withered little hand in his, as if he wished to keep him by his side, and dreaded that he might be taken from him.

"Tell me if Tiny Tim will live," said Scrooge, with an interest he had never felt before. "I hope will live."

"I see a vacant seat," replied the Ghost, "in the poor chimney corner, and a crutch without an owner, carefully preserved. If these shadows remain unaltered by the Future, the child will die."

"No, no," said Scrooge. "Oh no, kind Spirit! say he will be spared!"

"If these shadows remain unaltered by the Future, none other of my race," returned the Ghost, "will find him here. What then? If he be like to die, he had better do it, and decrease the surplus population."

Scrooge hung his head to hear his own words quoted by the Spirit, and was overcome with penitence and grief.

"Man!" said the Ghost, "if man you be in heart, not adamant, forbear that wicked cant until you have discovered what the surplus is, and where it is. Will you decide what men shall live, what men shall die? It may be, that in the sight of Heaven, you are more worthless and less fit to live than millions like this poor man's child. Oh God! to hear the Insect on the leaf pronouncing on the too much life among his hungry brothers in the dust!"

Scrooge bent before the Ghost's rebuke, and trembling cast his eyes upon the ground. But he raised them speedily, on hearing his own name.

"Mr Scrooge!" said Bob; "I'll give you Mr Scrooge, the Founder of

had had her doubts about the quantity of flour. Everybody had something to say about it, but nobody said or thought it was at all a small pudding for a large family. It would have been flat heresy to do so. Any Cratchit would have blushed to hint at such a thing.

At last the dinner was all done; the cloth was cleared, the hearth swept, and the fire made up. The compound in the jug being tasted and considered perfect, apples and oranges were put upon the table, and a shovel full of chestnuts on the fire. Then all the Cratchit family drew round the hearth, in what Bob Cratchit called a circle—meaning half a one—and at Bob Cratchit's elbow, stood the family display of glass: two tumblers, and a custard cup without a handle.

These held the hot stuff from the jug, however, as well as golden goblets would have done; and Bob served it out with beaming looks, while the chestnuts on the fire, sputtered and crackled noisily. Then Bob proposed:

"A Merry Christmas to us all, my dears. God bless us!"

Which all the family re-echoed.

"God bless us every one!" said Tiny Tim, the last of all.

He sat very close to his father's side upon his little stool. Bob held his withered little hand in his, as if he loved the child, and wished to keep him by his side, and dreaded that he might be taken from him.

"Spirit," said Scrooge, with an interest he had never felt before. "Tell me if Tiny Tim will live."

"I see a vacant seat," replied the Ghost, "in the poor chimney corner, and a crutch, without an owner, carefully preserved. The child will die."

"No no," said Scrooge. "Oh no, kind Spirit! Say he will be spared."

"None other of my race," returned the Ghost, "will find him here. What then? If he be like to die, he had better do it, and decrease the surplus population."

Scrooge hung his head to hear his own words quoted by the Spirit, and was somewhat overcome with penitence and grief.

"Man!" said the Ghost, "if man you be in heart; not adamant; forbear that wicked cant until you have discovered What the surplus is, and Where it is. Will you and such as you decide what men shall live, what men shall die! It may be, that in the sight of Heaven, you are more worthless and less fit to live than millions like this poor man's child. Oh God, to hear the Insect on the leaf, pronouncing on the too much life among his hungry brothers in the dust!"

Scrooge bent before the Ghost's rebuke, and, trembling cast, his eyes upon the ground. But he raised them speedily, on hearing his own name.

"Mr. Scrooge!" said Bob. "I'll give you Mr. Scrooge, the Founder of the Feast!"

"The Founder of the Feast indeed!" cried Mrs Cratchit, reddening. "I wish I had him here. I'd give him a piece of my mind to feast upon, and I hope he'd have a good appetite for it."

"My dear" said Bob: "the children — christmas Day."

"It should be christmas Day, I am sure," said she, "on which one drinks the health of such an odious, stingy, hard, unfeeling man as Mr Scrooge. You know he is, Robert! Nobody knows it better than you do, poor fellow!"

"My dear," was Bob's mild answer. "christmas Day."

"He drink his health for your sake and the Day's," said Mrs Cratchit. "not for his. Long life to him! a merry christmas and a happy new year — he'll be very merry and very happy I have no doubt!"

The children drank the toast after her. It was the first of their proceedings which had no heartiness in it. Tiny Tim drank it last of all, but he didn't care two pence for it. Scrooge was the Ogre of the family. The mention of his name cast a dark shadow on the party which was not dispelled for full five minutes.

After it had passed away, they were ten times merrier than before from the mere relief of Scrooge the Baleful being done with. Bob Cratchit told them how he had a situation in his eye for Master Peter, which would bring in, if obtained, full five and sixpence weekly. The two young Cratchits laughed tremendously at the idea of Peter's being a man of business; and Peter himself looked at the fire from between his collars, as if he were deliberating what particular Investments he should favor, when it came into his head receipt of that unwedding Income. Martha, who was a poor apprentice at a milliners then told them what kind of work she had to do, and how many hours she worked at a stretch, and how she meant to lie abed tomorrow morning for a good long rest — tomorrow being a holiday she passed at home. Also she had seen a countess and a lord some days before, and how the lord "was much about as tall as Peter"; at which Peter pulled up his collars so high, that you couldn't have seen his head if you had been there. All this time the chestnuts and the jug went round and round; and by and by they had a song from Tiny Tim, who had a plaintive little voice, and sang it very well indeed.

There was nothing of high mark in this; they were not a handsome family; they were not well dressed; their shoes were far from being waterproof; their clothes were scant; and might have known, and very likely did, the inside of a pawnbroker's. But they were happy, grateful, pleased with one another, and contented with the time; and when they faded, and looked happier yet in the bright

the Feast!"

"The Founder of the Feast indeed!" cried Mrs. Cratchit, reddening. "I wish I had him here. I'd give him a piece of my mind to feast upon, and I hope he'd have a good appetite for it."

"My dear," said Bob— "the children—Christmas Day."

"It should be Christmas Day, I am sure," said she, "on which one drinks the health of such an odious, stingy, hard, unfeeling man as Mr. Scrooge. You know he is, Robert! Nobody knows it better than you do, poor fellow!"

"My dear," was Bob's mild answer. "Christmas Day."

"I'll drink his health for your sake and the Day's," said Mrs. Cratchit, "not for his. Long life to him! A Merry Christmas and a happy New Year!—he'll be very merry and very happy I have no doubt!"

The children drank the toast after her. It was the first of their proceedings which had no heartiness in it. Tiny Tim drank it last of all, but he didn't care twopence for it. Scrooge was the ogre of the family. The mention of his name cast a dark shadow on the party which was not dispelled for full five minutes.

After it had passed away, they were ten times merrier than before, from the mere relief of Scrooge the Baleful being done with. Bob Cratchit told them how he had a situation in his eye for Master Peter, which would bring in, if obtained, full five and sixpence weekly. The two young Cratchits laughed tremendously at the idea of Peter's being a man of business; and Peter himself looked thoughtfully at the fire from between his collars, as if he were deliberating what particular investments he should favor when he came into the receipt of that bewildering Income. Martha, who was a poor apprentice at a milliners then told them what kind of work she had to do, and how many hours she worked at a stretch, and how she meant to lie abed tomorrow morning for a good long rest—tomorrow being a holiday she passed at home. Also, how she had seen a Countess and a Lord some days before, and how the Lord "was much about as tall as Peter"; at which Peter pulled up his collars so high, that you couldn't have seen his head if you had been there. All this time the chestnuts and the jug went round and round; and bye and bye they had a song, about a lost child travelling in the snow, from Tiny Tim; who had a plaintive little voice, and sang it very well indeed.

There was nothing of high mark in this; they were not a handsome family; they were not well dressed; their shoes were far from being waterproof; their clothes were scant; and Peter might have known, and very likely did, the inside of a Pawnbroker's. But they were happy, grateful, pleased with one another, and contented with the time; and when they faded, and looked happier yet in the bright sprinklings of the Spirit's torch at parting; Scrooge had his eye upon them, and specially on Tiny Tim, until the last.

By this time it was getting dark, and snowing pretty heavily; and as Scrooge and the Spirit went along the streets, the pies at bakers, parlors, and all sorts of rooms, was wonderful. Here the flickering of the blaze showed preparations for a cosy dinner, with not plates baking through and through before the fire, and deep red curtains ready to shut out cold and darkness. There all the children of the house were running out into the snow to meet the married sisters, brothers, cousins, uncles, aunts, and be the first to greet them. Here again were shadows on the window-blind of guests assembling; and there hooded and fur-booted; and all chattering at once, tripped lightly off to some near neighbour's house; where is upon the man who saw them enter or their way to friend gatherings you might have thought that no one was at home to give them welcome when they got there, instead of every house expecting company and piling up its fires half-chimney high.. hearth of heart, and opened his capacious and floated on, out pouring with a generous hand, bright and harmless fire on within rich! The very lamplighter who ran on before speaks of light was cheered to the snow laughed out loud, as the Spirit passed: though little the lamplighter that he had any company but Christmas!

And now, without a word of warning from the Spirit, they stood upon a bleak and desert moor where masses of rude stone were cast about, and water spread itself wheresoever it listed — or would have done so, but for the frost that held it prisoner, and nothing grew but moss and furze, and coarse rank grass. In the West the setting sun had left a streak of fiery red, which upon the desolation for an instant, like a sullen eye, and lower lower yet, was lost in the thick of darkest night.

"What place is this?" asked Scrooge.

"A place where miners live, who labour in the bowels of the earth," returned the Spirit. "But they know me. See!"

A light shone from the window of a hut, they advanced towards it. Passing through the wall of mud and stone, they found a cheerful company assembled round a glowing fire.

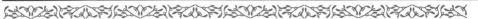

sprinklings of the Spirit's torch at parting; Scrooge had his eye upon them, and especially on Tiny Tim, until the last.

By this time it was getting dark, and snowing pretty heavily; and as Scrooge and the Spirit went along the streets, the brightness of the roaring fires in kitchens, parlors, and all sorts of rooms, was wonderful. Here, the flickering of the blaze shewed preparations for a cosy dinner, with hot plates baking through and through before the fire, and deep red curtains ready to be drawn to shut out cold and darkness. There all the children of the house were running out into the snow to meet the married sisters, brothers, cousins, uncles, aunts, and be the first to greet them. Here again, were shadows on the window-blind of guests assembling; and there, a group of handsome girls, all hooded and fur-booted and all chattering at once, tripped lightly off to some near neighbour's house; where, wo upon the single man who saw them enter—artful witches; well they knew it—in a glow!

But if you had judged from the numbers of people on their way to friendly gatherings, you might have thought that no one was at home to give them welcome when they got there, instead of every house expecting company, and piling up its fires half chimney high. Blessings on it, how the Ghost exulted! How it swung its torch, and bared its breadth of breast, and opened its capacious palm, and floated on, outpouring, with a generous hand, its bright and harmless fire on everything within its reach! The very lamplighter, who ran on before dotting the dusky street with specks of light, and who was dressed to spend the evening somewhere, laughed out loudly, as the Spirit passed: though little kenned the Lamplighter that he had any company but Christmas!

And now, without a word of warning from the Ghost, they stood upon a bleak and desert moor, where monstrous masses of rude stone were cast about, as though it were the burial-place of giants; and water spread itself wheresoever it listed—or would have done so, but for the frost that held it prisoner—and nothing grew but moss and furze, and coarse rank grass. Down in the West the setting sun had left a streak of fiery red, which glared upon the desolation for an instant, like a sullen eye, and frowning lower, lower, lower yet, was lost in the thick gloom of darkest night.

"What place is this?" asked Scrooge.

"A place where miners live, who labour in the bowels of the Earth," returned the Spirit. "But they know me. See!"

A light shone from the window of a hut, and swiftly they advanced towards it. Passing through the wall of mud and stone, they found a cheerful company assembled round a glowing fire. An old, old man and woman, with their children, and

all decked out gaily in their holiday attire:
their children's children, and another generation beyond that: The old man, in a voice
that seldom rose above the howling of the wind upon the barren waste, was
singing them a christmas song — it had been a very old song when he was a
boy; and from time to time they all joined in the chorus. So surely as they raised
their voices, the old man got quite blithe and loud; and so surely as they stopped, his
vigour sank again.

The Spirit did not tarry here, but bade Scrooge hold his robe, and
passing on above the moor, sped — whither? Not to sea? To sea. To Scrooge's horror, looking back,
he saw the last of the land, a frightful range of rocks, behind them; and his ears were deafened
by the thundering of water, as it rolled and roared and raged among the dreadful
caverns it had worn, and fiercely tried to undermine the Earth.

Built upon a dismal reef of sunken rocks,
some league or so from shore, on
which the waters chafed and dashed, the wild year through, there stood
a solitary lighthouse. Great heaps of seaweed clung to its base, and
storm birds — born of the wind one might suppose, as seaweed of the water —
rose and fell about it, like the waves they skimmed.

But even here, two men who watched the light had made a fire that
through the loophole in the thick stone wall, shed out a ray of brightness on the
awful sea. Joining their horny hands over the rough table at which
they sat, they wished each other merry christmas in their can of grog; and one
of them — the elder too, with his face all damaged and scarred with hard weather
like the figure head of an old ship — struck up a sturdy song that was like
a Gale in itself.

Again the Ghost sped on, above the black and heaving sea
— on, on — until, being far away, as he told Scrooge, from any shore, they lighted
on a Ship. They stood beside the helmsman at the wheel, the look-out in the bow, the officers
who had the watch; dark, ghostly figures in their several stations;
but every man among them hummed a christmas tune, or had a christmas thought, or spoke below his breath to his companion of some bygone christ-
mas Day, with homeward hopes belonging to it. And every man on board, waking or sleeping, good or bad, had had a
kinder word for another on that day than on any day in the year; and
had shared to some extent in its festivities, and had remembered those he cared for at a distance,
and known that they delighted to remember him.

It was a great surprise to Scrooge while listening to the
moaning of the winds, and thinking what a solemn thing it was to move on
through the lonely darkness over an unknown abyss, whose depths were secrets
as profound as death — it was a great surprise to Scrooge while thus engaged
to hear a hearty laugh. It was a much greater surprise to Scrooge
to recognise it as his own nephew's, and to find himself in a bright dry
gleaming room, with the Spirit standing smiling by his side,
and looking at that same nephew with approving affability!

their children's children, and another generation beyond that: all decked out gaily in their holiday attire. The old man in a voice that seldom rose above the howling of the wind upon the barren waste, was singing them a Christmas song—it had been a very old song when he was a boy—and from time to time they all joined in the chorus. So surely, they raised their voices, the old man got quite blithe and loud; and so surely as they stopped, his vigour sank again.

The Spirit did not tarry here, but bade Scrooge hold his robe, and passing on above the moor, sped whither—Not to sea? To sea. To Scrooge's horror, looking back he saw the last of the land—a frightful range of rocks—behind them; and his ears were deafened by the thundering of water, as it rolled and roared and raged among the dreadful caverns it had worn, and fiercely tried to undermine the earth.

Built upon a dismal reef of sunken rocks, some league or so from shore, on which the waters chafed and dashed, the wild year through, there stood a solitary lighthouse. Great heaps of seaweed clung to its base, and storm birds—born of the wind one might suppose, as seaweed of the water—rose and fell about it, like the waves they skimmed.

But even here, two men who watched the light had made a fire that through the loophole in the thick stone wall, shed out a ray of brightness on the awful sea. Joining their horny hands over the rough table at which they sat, they wished each other Merry Christmas in their can of grog; and one of them—the elder, too, with his face all damaged and scarred with hard weather as the figurehead of an old ship might be—struck up a sturdy song that was like a Gale in itself.

Again the Ghost sped on, above the black and heaving sea—on, on—until, being far away as he told Scrooge, from any shore, they lighted on a ship. They stood beside the helmsman at the wheel, the look-out in the bow, the officers who had the watch; dark, ghostly figures in their several stations; but every man among them hummed a Christmas tune, or had a Christmas thought, or spoke below his breath to his companion of some bygone Christmas Day, with homeward hopes belonging to it. And every man on board, waking or sleeping, good or bad, had had a kinder word for another on that day than on any day in the year; and had shared to some extent in its festivities, and had remembered those he cared for at a distance; and had known that they delighted to remember him.

It was a great surprise to Scrooge, while listening to the moaning of the wind, and thinking what a solemn thing it was to move on through the lonely darkness over an unknown abyss, whose depths were secrets as profound as Death—it was a great surprise to Scrooge while thus engaged, to hear a hearty laugh. It was a much greater surprise to Scrooge to recognize it as his own nephew's, and to find himself in a bright, dry, gleaming room with the Spirit standing smiling by his side and looking at that same nephew with approving affability!

43

"Ha ha!" "laughed Scrooge's nephew. "Ha ha ha!"

If you should happen, by any chance, to know a man more blest in a laugh than Scrooge's nephew, all I can say is I should like to know him too. Introduce him to me, and I'll cultivate his acquaintance. It is a fair, even handed, glorious adjustment of things that while there is infection in disease and sorrow, there is nothing in the world so irresistibly contagious as laughter and good-humour. When Scrooge's nephew laughed in this way — holding his sides, rolling his head, and twisting his face into the most extravagant contortions — Scrooge's niece, by marriage, laughed as heartily as he; and their assembled friends being not a whit behind-hand, roared out, lustily, "Ha ha! Ha ha ha ha!"

"He said that christmas was a humbug, as I live!" cried Scrooge's nephew. "He believed it too!"

"More shame for him, Fred!" said Scrooge's niece, indignantly. Bless those women, they never do anything by halves — They are always in earnest.

She was very pretty: exceedingly pretty. With a dimpled surprised-looking, capital face; a ripe little mouth that seemed made to be kissed — as no doubt it was; all kinds of good little dots about her chin that melted into one another when she laughed; and the sunniest pair of eyes you ever saw. Altogether she was what you would have called provoking you know; but satisfactory. Oh, perfectly satisfactory!

"He's a comical old fellow," said Scrooge's nephew "that's the truth; and not so pleasant as he might be. However, his offences carry their own punishment, and I have nothing to say against him."

"I'm sure he's very rich, Fred," hinted Scrooge's niece. "at least you always tell me so."

"What of that, my dear!" said Scrooge's nephew. "His wealth is of no use to him. He don't do any good with it. He don't make himself comfortable with it. He hasn't the satisfaction of thinking — ha ha ha — that he is ever going to benefit us with it."

"I have no patience with him," observed Scrooge's niece. Scrooge's niece's sisters, and all the other ladies expressed the same opinion.

"Oh, I have!" said Scrooge's nephew. "I am sorry for him; I couldn't be angry with him if I tried. Who suffers by his ill whims? Himself always. Here he takes it into his head to dislike us, and he won't come and dine with us. What's the consequence? He don't lose much of a dinner —"

"Indeed I think he loses a very good dinner," interrupted Scrooge's niece. Everybody else said the same, and they must be allowed to have been competent judges, because they had just had dinner; and with the dessert upon the table, were all clustered round the fire, by lamplight.

"Ha ha!" laughed Scrooge's nephew. "Ha ha ha!"

If you should happen by any unlikely chance to know a man more blest in a laugh than Scrooge's nephew, all I can say is, I should like to know him too. Introduce him to me, and I'll cultivate his acquaintance.

It is a fair, even handed glorious adjustment of things that while there is infection in disease and sorrow, there is nothing in the world so irresistibly contagious as laughter and good-humour. When Scrooge's nephew laughed in this way—holding his sides, rolling his head, and twisting his face into the most extravagant contortions—Scrooge's niece by marriage, laughed as heartily as he; and their assembled friends being not a bit behind-hand, roared out, lustily.

"Ha ha! Ha ha ha ha!"

"He said that Christmas was a humbug, as I live!" cried Scrooge's nephew. "He believed it too!"

"More shame for him, Fred!" said Scrooge's niece, indignantly. Bless those women; they never do anything by halves. They are always in earnest.

She was very pretty, exceedingly pretty. With a dimpled, surprised-looking, capital face; a dainty little mouth that seemed made to be kissed—as no doubt it was; all kinds of good little dots about her chin, that melted into one another when she laughed; and the sunniest pair of eyes you ever saw in any little creature's head. Altogether she was what you would have called provoking, you know, but satisfactory, too. Oh, perfectly satisfactory!

"He's a comical old fellow," said Scrooge's nephew, "that's the truth: and not so pleasant as he might be. However, his offences carry their own punishment, and I have nothing to say against him."

"I'm sure he's very rich, Fred," hinted Scrooge's niece. "At least you always tell *me* so."

"What of that, my dear!" said Scrooge's nephew. "His wealth is of no use to him. He don't do any good with it. He don't make himself comfortable with it. He hasn't the satisfaction of thinking—ha ha ha!—that he is ever going to benefit us with it."

"I have no patience with him," observed Scrooge's niece. Scrooge's niece's sisters, and all the other ladies, expressed the same opinion.

"Oh! I have." said Scrooge's nephew. "I am sorry for him. I couldn't be angry with him if I tried. Who suffers by his ill whims? Himself always. Here he takes it into his head to dislike us, and he won't come and dine with us. What's the consequence? He don't lose much of a dinner—"

"Indeed I think he loses a very good dinner," interrupted Scrooge's niece. Everybody else said the same, and they must be allowed to have been competent judges, because they had just had dinner; and, with the dessert upon the table, were clustered round the fire, by lamplight.

44

I haven't any great faith in these

"Well! I am very glad to hear it," said Scrooge's nephew, "because young house-keepers ... you say, Topper."

Topper had clearly got his eye on one of Scrooge's niece's sisters, for he answered that a bachelor was a wretched outcast, who had no right ... Scrooge's niece's sister — the plump one, not the one with the roses — blushed.

"Do go on, Fred," said Scrooge's niece, clapping her hands. "He never finishes what he begins to say! He is such a ridiculous fellow!"

Scrooge's nephew ... and as it was impossible to keep the infection off — though the plump sister tried hard to do it with aromatic vinegar — was unanimously followed.

"I was going to say," said Scrooge's nephew, "that the consequence of his taking a dislike to us, and not making merry with us, as I think, that he loses some pleasant moments ... I am sure he loses pleasanter companions than he can find in his own thoughts, either in his mouldy old office or his dusty chambers ... for I pity him ... He may rail at Christmas till he dies, but he can't help thinking better of it — I defy him — if he finds me going there, in good humor, year after year, and saying uncle Scrooge, how are you? If it only puts him in the vein to leave his poor clerk fifty pounds, that's something. And I think I shook him yesterday."

It was their turn to laugh now, at the notion of his shaking Scrooge. But being thoroughly good-natured, and not much caring what they laughed at, so that they laughed at any rate, he encouraged them in their merriment, and passed the bottle, joyously.

After tea, they had some music. For they were a musical family, and knew what they were about, when they sang a glee or catch, I can assure you — especially Topper who could growl away in the bass like a good one, and never swell the veins in his forehead, or get red in the face over it. Scrooge's niece played well upon the harp; and played among other tunes a simple little air (a mere nothing: you might learn to whistle it in two minutes) which had been familiar to the child who fetched Scrooge from the boarding-school, as he had been reminded by the Ghost of Christmas Past. When this music came upon him, all the things the Ghost had shown him, came upon his mind; he softened more and more; and thought that if he could have listened to it often, years ago, he might have cherished the kindnesses of life for his own happiness with his own hands, without ... Jacob Marley ...

But they didn't devote the whole evening to music. After a while they played at forfeits; for it is good to be children sometimes, and never

"Well! I am very glad to hear it," said Scrooge's nephew, "because I haven't great faith in these young housekeepers. What do *you* say, Topper?"

Topper had clearly got his eye upon one of Scrooge's niece's sisters, for he answered that a bachelor was a wretched outcast, who had no right to express an opinion on the subject. Whereat, Scrooge's niece's sister—the plump one with the lace tucker; not the one with the roses—blushed.

"Do go on, Fred," said Scrooge's niece, clapping her hands. "He never finishes what he begins to say! He is such a ridiculous fellow!"

Scrooge's nephew revelled in another laugh, and as it was impossible to keep the infection off—though the plump sister tried hard to do it with aromatic vinegar—his example was unanimously followed.

"I was only going to say," said Scrooge's nephew, "that the consequence of his taking a dislike to us, and not making merry with us, is, as I think, that he loses some pleasant moments, which could do him no harm. I am sure he loses pleasanter companions than he can find in his own thoughts, either in his mouldy old office or his dusty chambers. I mean to give him the same chance every year, whether he likes it or not, for I pity him. He may rail at Christmas till he dies, but he can't help thinking better of it—I defy him—if he finds me going there, in good temper, year after year, and saying Uncle Scrooge, how are you. If it only puts him in the vein to leave his poor clerk fifty pounds, *that's* something. And I think I shook him, yesterday."

It was their turn to laugh now, at the notion of his shaking Scrooge. But being thoroughly good-natured, and not much caring what they laughed at, so that they laughed at any rate, he encouraged them in their merriment, and passed the bottle, joyously.

After tea, they had some music. For they were a musical family, and knew what they were about, when they sung a glee or catch, I can assure you—especially Topper who could growl away in the bass like a good one, and never swell the large vein in his forehead or get red in the face over it. Scrooge's niece played well upon the Harp; and played among other tunes a simple little air (a mere nothing: you might learn to whistle it in two minutes) which had been familiar to the child who fetched Scrooge from the boarding-school, as he had been reminded by the Ghost of Christmas Past. When this strain of music sounded, all the things that Ghost had shewn him, came upon his mind; he softened more and more; and thought that if he could have listened to it often, years ago, he might have cultivated the kindnesses of life, on his own happiness with his own hands, without resorting to the sexton's spade that buried Jacob Marley.

But they didn't devote the whole evening to music. After a while they played at forfeits; for it is good to be children sometimes, and never better than at christmas, when its mighty founder was a child himself. There was first a game at blindman's buff. Of course there was. And I no more believe Topper was really blind than I believe he had eyes in his boots. My opinion is, that it was a done thing between him and Scrooge's nephew, and that the Ghost of christmas Present knew it. The way he went after that plump sister in the lace tucker, was an outrage on the credulity of human nature. Knocking down the fire irons, tumbling over the chairs, bumping up against the piano, smothering himself among the curtains, wherever she went, there went he. He always knew where the plump sister was. He wouldn't catch anybody else. If you had fallen up against him, as some of them did, and stood there, he would have made a feint of endeavouring to seize you, which would have been an affront to your understanding; and would instantly have sidled off in the direction of the plump sister. She often cried out that it wasn't fair, and it really was not. But when at last, he caught her; when, in spite of all her silken rustlings, and her rapid flutterings past him, he got her into a corner whence there was no escape; then his conduct was the most execrable. For his pretending not to know her; his pretending that it was necessary to touch her head dress, and further to assure himself of her identity by pressing a certain ring upon her finger, and a certain chain about her neck; was vile, monstrous! No doubt she told him her opinion of it, when, another blind man being in office, they were so very confidential together, behind the curtains. Scrooge's niece was not one of the blind man's buff party, but was made comfortable with a large chair and a footstool, in a snug corner, where the Ghost and Scrooge were close behind her. But she joined in the forfeits, and loved her love to admiration with all the letters of the alphabet. Likewise at the game of how, when, and where, she was very great, and to the secret joy of Scrooge's nephew, beat her sisters hollow — though they were sharp girls too, as Topper could have told you. There might have been twenty people there, young and old, but they all played, and so did Scrooge; for wholly forgetting in the interest he had in what was going on, that his voice made no sound in their ears, he sometimes came out with his guess quite loud, and very often guessed right too, for the sharpest needle, best Whitechapel, warranted not to cut in the eye — was not sharper than Scrooge; blunt as he took it in his head to be.

The Ghost was greatly pleased to find him in this mood, and looked upon him with such favor, that he begged like a boy to be allowed to stay until the guests departed. But this the Spirit said, could not be done.

"Here's a new game," said Scrooge. "one half hour, Spirit, only one!"

better than at Christmas, when its mighty founder was a child Himself. Stop! There was first a game at blindman's buff. Of course there was. And I no more believe Topper was really blind than I believe he had eyes in his boots. My opinion is, that it was a done thing between him and Scrooge's nephew, and that the Ghost of Christmas Present knew it. The way he went after that plump sister in the lace tucker, was an outrage on the credulity of human nature. Knocking down the fire irons, tumbling over the chairs, bumping against the piano, smothering himself among the curtains, wherever she went, there went he. He always knew where the plump sister was. He wouldn't catch anybody else. If you had fallen up against him, as some of them did; and stood there; he would have made a feint of endeavouring to seize you, which would have been an affront to your understanding; and would instantly have sidled off in the direction of the plump sister. She often cried out that it wasn't fair; and it really was not. But when at last, he caught her; when, in spite of all her silken rustlings, and her rapid flutterings past him, he got her into a corner whence there was no escape; then his conduct was the most execrable. For his pretending not to know her; his pretending that it was necessary to touch her headdress, and further to assure himself of her identity by pressing a certain ring upon her finger and a certain chain about her neck; was vile, monstrous! No doubt she told him her opinion of it, when, another blindman being in office, they were so very confidential together, behind the curtains.

Scrooge's niece was not one of the blindman's buff party, but was made comfortable, with a large chair and a footstool, in a snug corner, where the Ghost and Scrooge were close behind her. But she joined in the forfeits, and loved her lord to admiration with all the letters of the alphabet. Likewise at the game of How, When, and Where, she was very great, and to the secret joy of Scrooge's nephew, beat her sisters hollow—though they were sharp girls too, as Topper could have told you. There might have been twenty people there, young and old, but they all played, and so did Scrooge; for wholly forgetting in the interest he had in what was going on, that his voice made no sound in their ears, he sometimes came out with his guess quite loud, and very often guessed quite right too, for the sharpest needle—best Whitechapel, warranted not to cut in the eye—was not sharper than Scrooge: blunt as he took it in his head to be.

The Ghost was greatly pleased to find him in this mood, and looked upon him with such favor that he begged, like a boy, to be allowed to stay until the guests departed. But this the Spirit said, could not be done.

"Here's a new game," said Scrooge. "One half hour, Spirit, only one!"

46

It was a game called Yes and no, where Scrooge's nephew had to think of something, and the rest must find out what: he only answering to their questions yes or no, as the case was. The brisk fire of questioning to which he was exposed, elicited from him that he was thinking of an animal, a live animal, rather a disagreeable animal, a savage animal, an animal that growled and grunted sometimes, and talked sometimes, and lived in London and walked about the streets, and wasn't made a show of, and wasn't led by anybody, and didn't live in a menagerie, and was never killed in a market, and was not a horse, or an ass, or a cow, or a bull, or a tiger, or a dog, or a pig, or a cat, or a bear. At every fresh question that was put to him, this nephew burst into a fresh roar of laughter; and was so inexpressibly tickled that he was obliged to get up off the sofa, and stamp. At last the plump sister, falling into a similar state, cried out:

"I have found it out! I know what it is, Fred! I know what it is!"

"What is it!" cried Fred.

"It's your Uncle Scro-o-o-o-oge!"

Which it certainly was. Admiration was the universal sentiment, though some objected that the reply to "Is it a Bear?" ought to have been "Yes"; inasmuch as an answer in the negative was sufficient to have diverted their thoughts from Mr Scrooge, supposing they had ever had any tendency that way.

"He has given us plenty of merriment, I am sure," said Fred, "and it would be ungrateful not to drink his health. Here is a glass of mulled wine ready to our hand at the moment; and I say 'Uncle Scrooge!'"

"Well! Uncle Scrooge!" they cried.

"A merry Christmas and a happy new year to the old man, whatever he is!" said Scrooge's nephew. "He wouldn't take it from me, but may have it, nevertheless. Uncle Scrooge!"

Uncle Scrooge had imperceptibly become so gay and light of heart, that he would have pledged the unconscious company in return, and thanked them in an inaudible speech, if the Ghost had given him time. But the whole scene passed off in the breath of the last word spoken by his nephew; and he and the Spirit were again upon their travels.

Much they saw, and far they went, and many homes they visited, but always with a happy end. The Spirit stood beside sick beds, and they were cheerful; on foreign lands, and they were close at home; by struggling men, and they were patient in their greater hope; by poverty, and it was rich. In almshouse

It was a game called Yes and No, where Scrooge's nephew had to think of something, and the rest must find out what: he only answering to their questions yes or no, as the case was. The brisk fire of questioning to which he was exposed, elicited from him that he was thinking of an animal, a live animal, rather a disagreeable animal, a savage animal, an animal that growled and grunted sometimes, and talked sometimes, and lived in London, and walked about the streets, and wasn't made a show of, and wasn't led by anybody, and didn't live in a menagerie, and was never killed in a market, and was not a horse, or an ass, or a cow, or a bull, or a tiger, or a dog, or a pig, or a cat, or a bear. At every fresh question that was put to him this nephew burst into a fresh roar of laughter, and was so inexpressibly tickled that he was obliged to get up, off the sofa, and stamp. At last the plump sister, falling into a similar state, cried out:

"I have found it out! I know what it is, Fred! I know what it is!"

"What is it!" cried Fred.

"It's your Uncle Scro-o-o-o-oge!"

Which it certainly was. Admiration was the universal sentiment, though some objected that the reply to "Is it a Bear?" ought to have been "Yes," inasmuch as an answer in the negative was sufficient to have diverted their thoughts from Mr. Scrooge, supposing that they had ever had any tendency that way.

"He has given us plenty of merriment, I am sure," said Fred, "and it would be ungrateful not to drink his health. Here is a glass of mulled wine ready to our hand at the moment; and I say 'Uncle Scrooge!' "

"Well! Uncle Scrooge!" they cried. ·

"A Merry Christmas and a Happy New Year to the old man, whatever he is!" said Scrooge's nephew. "He wouldn't take it from me, but may he have it, nevertheless. Uncle Scrooge!"

Uncle Scrooge had imperceptibly become so gay and light of heart, that he would have pledged the unconscious company in return, and thanked them in an inaudible speech, if the Ghost had given him time. But the whole scene passed off, in the breath of the last word spoken by his nephew; and he and the Spirit were again upon their travels.

Much they saw, and far they went, and many homes they visited, but always with a happy end. The Spirit stood beside sick beds, and they were cheerful; on foreign lands, and they were close at home; by struggling men, and they were patient in their greater hope; by Poverty, and it was rich. In almshouse

Hospitals, and Jails, in misery's every refuge, where vain man in his little brief authority had not made fast the door, and barred the Spirit out, he left his blessing, and taught Scrooge his precepts.

It was a long night, if it were only a night; but Scrooge had his doubts of this, because the Christmas Holydays appeared to be condensed into the space of time they passed together. It was strange too that while Scrooge remained unaltered, the Spirit remained unaltered in his outward form, the Ghost grew older, clearly older. Scrooge had observed this change, but never spoke of it, until they left a children's Twelfth Night party, when looking at the Spirit as they stood together in an open place, he noticed that its hair was grey.

"Are Spirits' lives so short?" asked Scrooge.

"My life upon this globe, is very brief", replied the Ghost. "It ends tonight."

"Tonight!" cried Scrooge.

"Tonight at midnight. Hark! The time is drawing near."

The chimes were ringing the three quarters past eleven, at that moment.

"Forgive me if I am not justified in what I ask", said Scrooge, looking intently at the Spirit's robe, "but I see it again — it's a foot! Not a claw!" "It might be a claw, for the flesh there is upon it", was the Spirit's sorrowful reply. "Look here."

From the folding of its robe, it brought two children; wretched, abject, frightful, hideous, miserable. They knelt down at its feet, and clung upon the outside of its garment.

"Oh Man! look here. Look, look, down here!" exclaimed the Ghost.

They were a boy and girl. Yellow, meagre, ragged, scowling, wolfish; but prostrate too in their humility. Where graceful youth should have filled their features out, and touched them with its freshest tints, a stale and shrivelled hand, like that of age, had pinched and twisted them, and pulled them into shreds. Where angels might have sat enthroned, devils lurked, and glared out menacing. No change, no degradation, no perversion of humanity, in any grade, through all the mysteries of wonderful creation, has monsters half so horrible and dread.

Scrooge started back, appalled.

Hospital, and Jail, in misery's every refuge, where vain man in his little brief authority had not made fast the door, and barred the Spirit out, he left his blessing, and taught Scrooge his precepts.

It was a long night, if it were only a night; but Scrooge had his doubts of this, because the Christmas Holydays appeared to be condensed into the space of time they passed together. It was strange too that while Scrooge remained unaltered in his outward form, the Ghost grew older, clearly older. Scrooge had observed this change, but never spoke of it, until they left a children's Twelfth Night party, when, looking at the Spirit as they stood together in an open place, he noticed that its hair was grey.

"Are Spirits' lives so short?" asked Scrooge.

"My life upon this globe, is very brief," replied the Ghost. "It ends tonight."

"Tonight!" cried Scrooge.

"Tonight at midnight. Hark! The time is drawing near."

The chimes were ringing the Three quarters past Eleven at that moment.

"Forgive me if I am not justified in what I ask," said Scrooge, looking intently at the Spirit's robe, "but—I see it again—it's a foot. Not a claw!"

"It might be a claw for the flesh there is upon it," was the Spirit's sorrowful reply. "Look here."

From the foldings of its robe, it brought two children; wretched, abject, frightful, hideous, miserable. They knelt down at its feet, and clung upon the outside of its garment.

"Oh Man! look here. Look, look, down here!" exclaimed the Ghost.

They were a boy and a girl. Yellow, meagre, ragged, scowling, wolfish but prostrate too in their humility. Where graceful youth should have filled their features out, and touched them with its freshest tints, a stale and shrivelled hand, like that of age, had pinched and twisted them and pulled them into shreds. Where angels might have sat enthroned, devils lurked, and glared out menacing. No change, no degradation, no perversion of humanity, in any grade, through all the mysteries of wonderful creation, has monsters half so horrible and dread.

Scrooge started back, appalled. Having them shewn to him in this way, he tried to say, they were fine children,

but the words choked themselves, ~~rather~~ rather than be parties to a lie of so of
such enormous magnitude.

"Spirit! are they yours?" Scrooge ~~could say no more~~ cried, say no more.

"They are Man's," said the Spirit, looking down upon them. "and they cling to
me ~~appealing~~ appealing from their fathers. This boy is Ignorance. This girl is
Want. Beware them both, and all of their degree, but most of all
beware this boy, for on his brow I see that written ~~is~~ ~~which~~ which is
~~Doom~~, unless the writing ~~be~~ erased. ~~Deny it!~~ "Deny it!" cried the Spirit,
stretching out its hand towards the city. "Slander those who tell it ye!
Admit it for your factious purposes, and make it worse! ~~And~~ ~~bide~~ the end!"

"Have they no refuge or resource?"

"~~Can nothing~~ for them?" cried Scrooge.

"Are they no Prisons?" said the Spirit, turning on him for the last time with
his own words. "are
there no Workhouses?"

The bell struck Twelve.

Scrooge ~~looked~~ looked about him for the Ghost, and saw it not. As
the last stroke ceased ~~to vibrate~~, he remembered the prediction of old
Jacob Marley, and ~~lifting up his eyes~~, beheld a solemn Phantom, draped
and hooded, coming like a mist along the ground, towards him.

children, but the words choked themselves, rather than be parties to a lie of such enormous magnitude.

"Spirit! are they yours?" Scrooge could say no more.

"They are Man's," said the Spirit, looking down upon them. "And they cling to me, appealing from their fathers. This boy is Ignorance. This girl is Want. Beware them both, and all of their degree, but most of all beware this boy, for on his brow I see that written which is Doom, unless the writing be erased. Deny it!" cried the Spirit, stretching out its hand towards the city. "Slander those who tell it ye! Admit it for your factious purposes, and make it worse! And bide the end!"

"Have they no refuge or resource?" cried Scrooge.

"Are there no Prisons?" said the Spirit, turning on him for the last time with his own words. "Are there no workhouses?"

The bell struck Twelve.

Scrooge looked about him for the Ghost, and saw it not. As the last stroke ceased to vibrate he remembered the prediction of old Jacob Marley, and lifting up his eyes, beheld a solemn phantom, draped and hooded, coming, like a mist along the ground, towards him.

49

Stave IV.

The Last of the Spirits.

The Phantom slowly, gravely, silently, approached. When it came near him, Scrooge bent down upon his knee; for in the very air through which this Spirit moved it seemed to scatter gloom and mystery.

It was shrouded in a deep black garment, which concealed its head, its face, its form, and left nothing of it visible, save one outstretched hand. But for this it would have been difficult to detach its figure from the night, and separate it from the darkness by which it was surrounded.

It was tall and stately when it came beside him, and its mysterious presence filled him with a solemn dread. He knew no more, for the Spirit neither spoke nor moved.

"I am in the presence of the Ghost of Christmas Yet To Come?" said Scrooge.

The Spirit answered not, but pointed onward with its hand.

"You are about to shew me shadows of the things that have not happened, but will happen in the time before us. Is that so, Spirit?"

The upper portion of the garment, was contracted for an instant in its folds, as if the Spirit had inclined its head. That was the only answer he received.

Although well used to ghostly company by this time Scrooge feared the silent shape so much, that his legs trembled beneath him, and he found he could hardly stand when he prepared to follow it. The Spirit paused a moment, as if observing his condition, and giving him time to recover.

But Scrooge was all the worse for this. It thrilled him with a vague uncertain horror, to know that behind the dusky shroud, there were ghostly eyes intently fixed upon him, while he, though he stretched his own to the utmost, could see nothing but a spectral hand, and one great heap of black.

"Ghost of the Future!" he exclaimed, "I fear you more than any Spectre I have seen. But, as I know your purpose is to do me good, and as I hope to live to be another man from what I was, I am prepared to bear you company, and do it with a thankful heart. Will you not speak to me?"

It gave him no reply. The hand was pointed straight before them.

"Lead on!" said Scrooge. "Lead on! The night is wearing fast away, and it is precious time to me, I know. Lead on, Spirit!"

STAVE IV.

The Last of the Spirits.

The Phantom slowly, gravely, silently, approached. When it came near him, Scrooge bent down upon his knee; for in the very air through which this Spirit moved, it seemed to scatter gloom, and mystery.

It was shrouded in a deep black garment, which concealed its head, its face, its form, and left nothing of it visible, save one outstretched hand. But for this, it would have been difficult to detach its figure from the night, and separate it from the darkness by which it was surrounded.

He felt that it was tall and stately, when it came beside him, and that its mysterious presence filled him with a solemn dread. He knew no more, for the Spirit neither spoke nor moved.

"I am in the presence of the Ghost of Christmas Yet To Come?" said Scrooge.

The Spirit answered not, but pointed onward with its hand.

"You are about to shew me, shadows of the things that have not happened, but will happen in the time before us," Scrooge pursued. "Is that so, Spirit?"

The upper portion of the garment was contracted for an instant in its folds, as if the Spirit had inclined its head. That was the only answer he received.

Although well used to ghostly company by this time, Scrooge feared the silent shape so much, that his legs trembled beneath him, and he found that he could hardly stand when he prepared to follow it. The Spirit paused a moment: as observing his condition, and giving him time to recover.

But Scrooge was all the worse for this. It thrilled him with a vague uncertain horror to know that behind the dusky shroud, there were ghostly eyes, intently fixed upon him, while he, though he stretched his own to the utmost, could see nothing but a spectral hand, and one great heap of black.

"Ghost of the Future!" he exclaimed. "I fear you more than any Spectre I have seen. But, as I know your purpose is to do me good; and as I hope to live to be another man from what I was: I am prepared to bear you company, and do it with a thankful heart. Will you not speak to me?"

It gave him no reply. The hand was pointed straight before them.

"Lead on!" said Scrooge. "Lead on. The night is waning fast, and it is precious time to me, I know. Lead on, Spirit!"

50

The Phantom moved away as it had come towards him, and Scrooge followed in the shadow of its dress, which bore him up, he thought, and carried him along.

They scarcely seemed to enter the city; for the city rather seemed to spring up about them, and encompass them of its own act. But there they were, in the heart of it; on 'change amongst the merchants; who hurried up and down, and chinked the money in their pockets, and conversed in groupes, and looked at their watches, and trifled thoughtfully with their great gold seals; and so forth; as Scrooge had seen them often.

The Spirit stopped beside one little knot of busing men. Observing that the hand was pointed to them, Scrooge advanced to listen to their talk.

"No," said a great fat man with a monstrous chin. "I don't know much about it, either way. I only know he's dead."

"When did he die?" enquired another.

"Last night, I believe."

"Why, what was the matter with him?" asked a third, taking a vast quantity of snuff out of a very large snuff-box. "I thought he'd never die."

"God knows," said the first with a yawn.

"What has he done with his money?" asked a red-faced gentleman with a pendulous excrescence on the end of his nose.

"I haven't heard," said the man with the large chin, yawning again. "Left it to his company, perhaps. He hasn't left it to me. That's all I know."

This pleasantry was received with a general laugh.

"It's likely to be a very cheap funeral," said the same speaker. "for upon my life I don't know of anybody to go to it. Suppose we make up a party and volunteer?"

"I don't mind going if a lunch is provided," observed the gentleman with the excrescence on his nose. "But I must be fed, if I make one."

Another laugh.

"Well! I am the most disinterested among you, after all," said the first speaker, "for I never wear black gloves, and I never eat lunches. But I'll offer to go, if anybody else will. When I come to think of it, I'm not at all sure that I wasn't his most particular friend; for we used to stop and speak whenever we met. Bye, bye!"

Speakers and listeners strolled away, and mixed with other groups. Scrooge looked for the Spirit for an explanation. He knew the men; and saw nothing very strange in this.

The phantom glided on into a street. Its finger pointed to two persons meeting. Scrooge listened again, thinking that the explanation might lie here.

He knew these men also, perfectly. They were men

The Phantom moved away as it had come towards him. Scrooge followed in the shadow of its dress, which bore him up, he thought, and carried him along.

They scarcely seemed to enter the city; for the city rather seemed to spring up about them, and encompass them, of its own act. But there they were, in the heart of it; on 'change amongst the merchants; who hurried up and down, and clinked the money in their pockets, and conversed in groupes, and looked at their watches, and trifled thoughtfully with their great gold seals; and so forth; as Scrooge had seen them often.

The Spirit stopped beside one little knot of business men. Observing that the hand was pointed to them, Scrooge advanced to listen to their talk.

"No," said a great fat man with a monstrous chin. "I don't know much about it, either way. I only know he's dead."

"When did he die?" inquired another.

"Last night, I believe."

"Why, what was the matter with him?" asked a third, taking a vast quantity of snuff out of a very large snuff-box. "I thought he'd never die."

"God knows," said the first, with a yawn.

"What has he done with his money?" asked a red-faced gentleman with a pendulous excrescence on the end of his nose, that shook like the gills of a Turkey-cock.

"I haven't heard," said the man with the large chin, yawning again. "Left it to his Company, perhaps. He hasn't left it to *me*. That's all I know."

This pleasantry was received with a general laugh.

"It's likely to be a very cheap funeral," said the same speaker, "for upon my life I don't know of anybody to go to it. Suppose we make up a party and volunteer."

"I don't mind going if a Lunch is provided," observed the gentleman with the excrescence on his nose. "But I must be fed, if I make one."

Another laugh.

"Well! I am the most disinterested among you, after all," said the first speaker, "for I never wear black gloves, and I never eat lunch. But I'll offer to go, if anybody else will. When I come to think of it, I'm not at all sure that I wasn't his most particular friend: for we used to stop and speak whenever we met. Bye, bye!"

Speakers and listeners strolled away, and mixed with the other group. Scrooge looked towards the Spirit for an explanation. He knew the men, and saw nothing very strange in this.

The phantom glided on into a street. Its finger pointed to two persons meeting. Scrooge listened again: thinking that the explanation might lie here.

He knew these men, also, perfectly. They were men

of business; very wealthy, and of great importance. He had made a point, always, of
standing well in their esteem — in a business point of view, strictly in a business
point of view.

"How are you?" said one

"How are you?" returned the other.

"Well!" said the first. "Old Scratch has got his own, at last, hey?"

"So I am told," returned the second. "Cold, isn't it?"

"Seasonable for christmas time. You're not a skaiter, I suppose?"

"No. No. Something else to think of. Good morning!"

Not another word. That was their meeting, their conversation, and their
parting.

Scrooge was at first inclined to be surprised that the Spirit should attach importance to conversations apparently so trivial; but feeling assured that they must have some
hidden purpose, he set himself to consider what it was likely to be. They could
scarcely be supposed to have any bearing on the death of Jacob, his old partner, for that was
Past, and this Ghost's province was the Future. Nor could he think of any one immediately connected with himself, to whom he could apply them. But no thing
doubting that to whomsoever they applied, they had some
latent moral for his own improvement, he resolved to treasure up
every word he heard and everything he saw: and especially to observe the shadow
of himself when it appeared. For he had an expectation
that the conduct of his future self would give him the clue he
missed and would render the solution of these
riddles easy.

He looked about in that very place for his own image;
but another man stood in his accustomed corner, and
though the clock pointed to his usual time of day for being there, he saw
no likeness of himself among the multitudes that poured in through
the Porch. It gave him little surprise, however, for he had been resolving
in his mind a change of life, and thought and hoped he saw his new-
born resolutions carried out in this.

Quiet and dark, beside him, stood the Phantom with its outstretched
hand. When he roused himself from his thoughtful quest he
fancied from the hand, and its situation in reference
to himself, that the Unseen eyes were looking at him keenly.
It made him shudder, and feel very cold.

They left the busy scene, and went into an obscure part of the
town, where Scrooge had never penetrated before, but recognised its situation and its bad repute. The ways were narrow; the
shops and houses wretched: the people half-naked, drunken, slipshod, ugly.
Alleys and archways, like so many cesspools, dis-
gorged their offences of smell, and dirt, and life, upon the straggling
streets; and the whole quarter

of business; very wealthy, and of great importance. He had made a point, always of standing well in their esteem—in a business point of view that is; strictly in a business point of view.

"How are you," said one.

"How are you," returned the other.

"Well!" said the first. "Old Scratch has got his own at last, hey?"

"So I am told," returned the second. "Cold isn't it?"

"Seasonable for Christmas time. You're not a skaiter, I suppose?"

"No. No. Something else to think of it. Good morning!"

Not another word. That was their meeting, their conversation, and their parting.

Scrooge was at first inclined to be surprised that the Spirit should attach importance to conversations apparently so trivial; but feeling assured that they must have some hidden purpose he set himself to consider what it was likely to be. They could scarcely be supposed to have any bearing on the death of Jacob, his old partner, for that was Past, and this Ghost's province was the Future. Nor could he think of any one immediately connected with himself, to whom he could apply them. But nothing doubting that to whomsoever they applied, they had some latent moral for his own improvement, he resolved to treasure up every word he heard, and everything he saw: and especially to observe the shadow of himself when it appeared. For he had an expectation that the conduct of his future self would give him the clue he missed and would render the solution of these riddles easy.

He looked about in that very place for his own image. But another man stood in his accustomed corner, and though the clock pointed to his usual time of day for being there, he saw no likeness of himself among the multitudes that poured in through the Porch. It gave him little surprise, however; for he had been revolving in his mind a change of life, and thought and hoped he saw his new-born resolutions carried out in this.

Quiet and dark beside him, stood the Phantom, with its outstretched hand. When he roused himself from his thoughtful quest, he fancied from the turn of the hand, and its situation in reference to himself, that the Unseen Eyes were looking at him keenly. It made him shudder, and feel very cold.

They left the busy scene, and went into an obscure part of the town, where Scrooge had never penetrated before, although he recognised its situation and its bad repute. The ways were foul and narrow; the shops and houses wretched; the people half-naked, drunken, slipshod, ugly. Alleys and archways, like so many cesspools, disgorged their offences of smell, and dirt, and life, upon the straggling streets; and the whole quarter reeked with crime, with filth, and misery.

Far in this den of infamous resort, there was a low-browed, beetling shop, below a pent-house roof, where iron, old rags, bottles, bones, and greasy offal, were bought. Upon the floor within, were piled up rusty keys, nails, chains, hinges, files, scales, weights, and refuse iron of all kinds. Secrets that few would like to scrutinise were bred and hidden in mountains of unseemly rags, masses of corrupted fat, and sepulchres of bones. Sitting in among the wares he dealt in, by a charcoal stove, made of old bricks, was a grey-haired rascal, nearly seventy years of age; who had screened himself from the cold air without, by a frousy curtaining of miscellaneous tatters, hung upon a line; and smoked his pipe in all the luxury of calm retirement.

Scrooge and the Phantom came into the presence of this man, just as a woman with a heavy bundle slunk into the shop. But she had scarcely entered, when another woman, similarly laden, came in too; and she was closely followed by a man in faded black, who was no less startled by the sight of them, than they had been upon the recognition of each other. After a short period of blank astonishment, in which the old man with the pipe had joined them, they all three burst into a laugh.

"Let the charwoman alone to be the first!" cried she who had entered first. "Let the laundress alone to be the second; and let the undertaker's man alone to be the third. Look here, old Joe, here's a chance! If we haven't all three met here, without meaning it!"

"You couldn't have met in a better place," said old Joe, removing his pipe from his mouth. "Come into the parlour. You were made free of it long ago, you know; and the other two an't strangers. Stop 'till I shut the door of the shop. Ah! How it skreeks! There an't such a rusty bit of metal in the place as its own hinges, I believe; and I'm sure there's no such old bones here, as mine. Ha, ha! We're all suitable to our calling, we're well matched. Come into the parlour. Come into the parlour."

The parlour was the space behind the screen of rags. The old man raked the fire together with an old stair-rod, and trimming his smoky lamp (for it was night) with the stem of his pipe, put it in his mouth again.

While he did this, the woman who had already thrown her bundle on the floor, sat down in a flaunting manner on a stool; crossing her elbows on her knees, and looking with a bold defiance at the other two.

"What odds then! What odds, Mrs Dilber!" said the woman. "Every person has a right to take care of themselves. He always did!"

"That's true, indeed!" said the laundress. "No man more so."

"Why then, don't stand staring as if you was afraid, woman; who's the wiser? We're not going to pick holes in each other's coats, I suppose?"

"No, indeed!" said Mrs Dilber. "We should hope not."

reeked with crime, with filth, and misery.

Far in this den of infamous resort, there was a low-browed, beetling shop, below a penthouse roof, where iron, old rags, bottles, bones, and greasy offal, were bought. Upon the floor within, were piled up heaps of rusty keys and nails, chains, hinges, files, scales, weights, and refuse iron of all kinds. Secrets that few would like to scrutinize were bred and hidden in mountains of unseemly rags, masses of corrupted fat, and sepulchres of bones. Sitting in among the wares he dealt in, by a charcoal stove, made of old bricks, was a grey-haired rascal, nearly seventy years of age, who had screened himself from the cold air without, by a frousy curtaining of miscellaneous tatters, hung upon a line; and smoked his pipe in all the luxury of calm retirement.

Scrooge and the Phantom came into the presence of this man, just as a woman with a heavy bundle slunk into the shop. But she had scarcely entered, when another woman, similarly laden, came in too; and she was closely followed by a man in faded black, who was no less startled by the sight of them, than they had been upon the recognition of each other. After a short period of blank astonishment, in which the old man with the pipe had joined them they all three burst into a laugh.

"Let the char-woman alone to be the first!" cried she who had entered first. "Let the laundress alone to be the second; and let the undertaker's man alone to be the third. Look here, old Joe, here's a chance. If we haven't all three met here without meaning it!"

"You couldn't have met in a better place," said old Joe, removing his pipe from his mouth. "Come into the parlor. You were made free of it long ago, you know; and the other two an't strangers. Stop 'till I shut the door of the shop. Ah! How it skreeks! There an't such a rusty bit of metal in the place as its own hinges, I believe; and I'm sure there's no such old bones here, as mine. Ha, ha! We're all suitable to our calling, we're well matched. Come into the parlor. Come into the parlor."

The parlor was the space behind the screen of rags. The old man raked the fire together with an old stair-rod and having trimmed his smoky lamp (for it was night) with the stem of his pipe, put it into his mouth again.

While he did this, the woman who had already spoken threw her bundle on the floor and sat down in a flaunting manner on a stool: crossing her elbows on her knees, and looking with a bold defiance at the other two.

"What odds then! What odds, Mrs. Dilber!" said the woman. "Every person has a right to take care of themselves. *He* always did!"

"That's true indeed!" said the laundress. "No man more so."

"Why, then don't stand staring as if you was afraid woman; who's the wiser. We're not going to pick holes in each other's coats, I suppose!"

"No, indeed!" said Mrs. Dilber and the man together. "We should hope not."

53

That's enough.

"Very well then!" cried the woman. "who's the worse for the loss of a few things like these? not a dead man, I suppose."

"No indeed," said Mrs Dilber, laughing.

"If he wanted to keep 'em after he was dead, a wicked old Screw," pursued the woman, "why wasn't he natural in his lifetime? If he had been, he'd have had somebody to look after him when he was struck with Death, instead of lying gasping out his last there, alone by himself."

"It's the truest word that ever was spoke," said Mrs Dilber. "It's a judgment on him."

"I wish it was a little heavier one," replied the woman, "and it should have been, you may depend upon it, if I could have laid my hands on anything else. Open that bundle, old Joe, and let me know the value of it. Speak out plain. I'm not afraid to be the first, nor afraid for them to see it. We knew pretty well that we were helping ourselves, before we met here, I believe. Open the bundle Joe."

But the gallantry of her friends would not allow of this; and the man in faded black, mounting the breach first, produced his plunder. It was not extensive. A seal or two, a pencil case, a pair of sleeve buttons, and a brooch of no great value, were all. They were severally examined and appraised by old Joe, who chalked the sums he was disposed to give upon the wall, and added them up into a total when he found that there was nothing more to come.

"That's your account," said Joe, "and I wouldn't give another sixpence, if I was to be boiled for not doing it. Who's next?"

Mrs Dilber was next. Sheets and towels, a little wearing apparel, two old fashioned silver teaspoons, a pair of sugar-tongs, and a few boots. Her account was stated on the wall in the same manner.

"I always give too much to ladies. It's a weakness of mine, and that's the way I ruin myself," said old Joe. "That's your account. If you asked me for another penny, and made it an open question, I'd repent of being so liberal and knock off half a crown."

"And now undo my bundle, Joe!" said the first woman.

Joe went down on his knees for the greater convenience of opening it, and having unfastened a great many knots, dragged out a large heavy roll of some dark stuff.

"What do you call this?" said Joe. "Bed curtains!"

"Ah!" returned the woman, laughing and leaning forward on her crossed arms. "Bed curtains!"

"You don't mean to say you took 'em down, rings and all, with him lying there?" said Joe.

"Yes I do," replied the woman. "Why not?"

"You were born to make your fortune," said Joe, "and you'll certainly do it."

"I certainly shan't hold my hand, when I can get anything in it by reaching it out, for the sake of a man as he was, I promise you, Joe," returned the woman coolly. "Don't drop

"Very well then!" cried the woman. "That's enough. Who's the worse for the loss of a few things like these? Not a dead man, I suppose."

"No, indeed," said Mrs. Dilber, laughing.

"If he wanted to keep 'em after he was dead, a wicked old screw," pursued the woman, "why wasn't he natural in his lifetime? If he had been, he'd have had somebody to look after him when he was struck with Death, instead of lying, gasping out his last there, alone by himself."

"It's the truest word that ever was spoke," said Mrs. Dilber. "It's a judgment on him."

"I wish it was a little heavier one," replied the woman, "and it should have been, you may depend upon it, if I could have laid my hands on anything else. Open that bundle, old Joe, and let me know the value of it. Speak out plain. I'm not afraid to be the first, nor afraid for them to see it. We know pretty well that we were helping ourselves, before we met here, I believe. It's no sin. Open the bundle Joe."

But the gallantry of her friends would not allow of this; and the man in faded black, mounting the breach first, produced his plunder. It was not extensive. A seal or two, a pencil-case, a pair of sleeve buttons, and a brooch of no great value, were all. They were severally examined and appraised by old Joe, who chalked the sums he was disposed to give for each upon the wall, and added them up into a total when he found there was nothing more to come.

"That's your account," said Joe, "and I wouldn't give another sixpence, if I was to be boiled for not doing it. Who's next?"

Mrs. Dilber was next. Sheets and towels, a little wearing apparel, two old-fashioned silver teaspoons, a pair of sugar-tongs, and a few boots. Her account was stated on the wall in the same manner.

"I always give too much to ladies. It's a weakness of mine, and that's the way I ruin myself," said old Joe. "That's your account. If you asked me for another penny, and made it an open question, I'd repent of being so liberal, and knock off half a crown."

"And now undo *my* bundle, Joe." said the first woman.

Joe went down on his knees for the greater convenience of opening it, and having unfastened a great many knots, dragged out a large and heavy roll of some dark stuff.

"What do you call this?" said Joe. "Bed curtains!"

"Ah!" returned the woman, laughing and leaning forward on her crossed arms. "Bed curtains!"

"You don't mean to say you took 'em down, rings and all, with him lying there?" said Joe.

"Yes I do," replied the woman. "Why not?"

"You were born to make your fortune," said Joe, "and you'll certainly do it."

"I certainly shan't hold my hand, when I can get anything in it by reaching it out, for the sake of such a man as He was I promise you Joe," returned the woman coolly. "Don't drop that oil upon the blankets."

"His blankets?" asked Joe.

"~~Whose else's~~ Whose else's do you think?" replied the woman. "He ~~isn't likely to take~~ cold ~~also~~ without 'em, ~~I dare say~~ I dare say."

"I hope he didn't die of anything catching? Eh?" said old Joe, stopping in his work, and cooking up.

"Don't you be afraid of that," returned the woman. "I an't so fond of his company, that ~~I'd loiter~~ I'd loiter about him for ~~the~~ such things, if he did. ah. You may cook through ~~that~~ the shirt 'till your eyes ache, but you won't find a hole in it, nor a ~~threadbare place~~ threadbare place. It's the best he had, and a fine one too. They'd have wasted it, if it hadn't been for me."

"what ~~do you~~ ~~nothing~~ call wasting of it?" asked old Joe.

"~~Putting~~ it on him to be buried in ~~the sure~~ ," replied the woman with a laugh. "~~Somebody~~ was fool enough to do it, but I took it off again. If calico an't ~~food~~ enough for ~~such purpose~~ , It isn't good enough for anything ~~it is~~ quite as becoming to the body. ~~I can dress~~ can't look ~~ugly~~ worse than ~~it did in that one~~ ."

~~Scrooge~~ listened to this dialogue in horror. As they ~~sat~~ gathered their spoil ~~gather~~ in the scanty light ~~afforded~~ ~~and~~ by the old man's lamp, he viewed them with ~~the~~ detestation ~~and disgust~~ ~~which could~~ hardly have been greater, ~~if~~ they had been ~~obscene~~ demons, ~~haggling~~ the corpse itself.

"Ha, ha!" laughed the same woman, when old Joe, producing a flannel bag with money in it, told out their several ~~fees~~ gains upon the ground. "This is the end of it, you see! He frightened every one away from him when he was alive, to profit us when he was dead! Ha ha ha!"

"Spirit!" said Scrooge, shuddering ~~from head to foot~~ ~~by my own~~ . "I see, I see. The case of this ~~unhappy~~ man might be ~~will~~ my l- kind, ~~this way, now~~ . Mer- ~~ciful Heaven, what is this~~ ."

He recoiled in terror, ~~for the~~ for ~~the scene had changed, and now~~ he almost touched a bed a bare uncurtained ~~bed, on which,~~ beneath a ragged sheet, there lay a something covered up, which ~~dumb as it was, in awful~~ announced itself in ~~fearful~~ language.

The room was very dark, too dark to be ~~observed~~ with any accuracy, though Scrooge ~~glanced round it~~ in ~~obedience to~~ a secret impulse ~~anxious~~ ~~to know~~ what kind of room it was. A pale light, rising ~~in~~ the outer air, fell straight upon the bed; and on it, plundered and bare, ~~unwatched~~ unwatched, unwept, uncared for, was the body of this man.

~~Scrooge glanced toward~~ the Phantom. ~~It's steady~~ hand was pointed to the head. The ~~coverlet was so carelessly adjusted that the slightest raising of it~~ ~~the faintest~~ motion of ~~a finger upon Scrooge's part~~ would have revealed the face. He thought of it, felt how easy it would be to do it, ~~and~~ longed to do it; but had no more power ~~to withdraw~~ the veil than to dismiss the Spectre at his side.

upon the blankets."

"His blankets?" asked Joe.

"Whose else's do you think?" replied the woman. "He isn't likely to take cold without 'em, I dare say."

"I hope he didn't die of anything catching? Eh?" said old Joe, stopping in his work, and looking up.

"Don't you be afraid of that," returned the woman. "I an't so fond of his company, that I'd loiter about him for such things, if he did. Ah! You may look through that shirt till your eyes ache; but you won't find a hole in it, nor a threadbare place. It's the best he had, and a fine one too. They'd have wasted it, if it hadn't been for me."

"What do you call wasting of it?" asked old Joe.

"Putting it on him to be buried in, to be sure," replied the woman with a laugh. "Somebody was fool enough to do it, but I took it off again. If calico an't good enough for such a purpose, it isn't good enough for anything. It's quite as becoming to the body. He can't look uglier than he did in that one."

Scrooge listened to this dialogue in horror. As they sat grouped about their spoil in the scanty light afforded by the old man's lamp, he viewed them with a detestation and disgust which could hardly have been greater, though they had been obscene demons, marketing the corpse itself.

"Ha ha!" laughed the same woman, when old Joe, producing a flannel bag with money in it, told out their several gains upon the ground. "This is the end of it, you see! He frightened every one away from him when he was alive, to profit us when he was dead! Ha ha ha!"

"Spirit!" said Scrooge, shuddering from head to foot. "I see, I see. The case of this unhappy man might be my own. My life tends that way, now. Merciful Heaven, what is this!"

He recoiled in terror, for the scene had changed, and now he almost touched a bed—a bare uncurtained bed—on which—beneath a ragged sheet, there lay a something covered up, which, though it was Dumb, announced itself in awful language.

The room was very dark, too dark to be observed with any accuracy, though Scrooge glanced round it in obedience to a secret impulse, anxious to know what kind of room it was. A pale light, rising in the outer air, fell straight upon the bed; and on it, plundered and bereft, unwatched, unwept, uncared for, was the body of this man.

Scrooge glanced towards the Phantom. Its steady hand was pointed to the head. The cover was so carelessly adjusted that the slightest raising of it: the motion of a finger upon Scrooge's part; would have revealed the face. He thought of it, felt how easy it would be to do, and longed to do it; but had no more power to withdraw the veil than to dismiss the Spectre at his side.

Oh cold, cold, rigid, dreadful Death, set up thy altar here, and dress it with such terrors as thou hast at thy command; for this is thy dominion. But of the loved, revered, and honored head, thou canst not turn one hair to thy dread purpose, or make one feature odious. It is not that the hand is heavy and will fall down when released; it is not that the heart and pulse are still; but that the hand was open, generous, and true; the heart brave, warm, and tender; and the pulse a man's. Strike, Shadow, strike! And see his good deeds springing from the wound, to sow the world with life immortal!

No voice pronounced these words in Scrooge's ears, and yet he heard them when he looked upon the bed. He thought, if this man could be raised up now, what would be his foremost thoughts? Avarice, hard dealing, griping cares? They have brought him to a rich end, truly!

He lay, in the dark empty house, with not a man, a woman, or a child to say, he was kind to me in this or that, and for the memory of one kind word, I will be kind to him. A cat was tearing at the door, and there was a sound of gnawing rats beneath the hearth stone. What they wanted in the room of death, and why they were so restless and disturbed, Scrooge did not dare to think.

"Spirit!" he said, "this is a fearful place. In leaving it, I shall not leave its lesson, trust me. Let us go!"

Still the Ghost pointed with an unmoving finger to the head.

"I understand you," Scrooge returned, "and I would do it, if I could. But I have not the power, Spirit. I have not the power."

Again it seemed to look upon him.

"If there is any person in the town, who feels emotion caused by this man's death," said Scrooge quite agonised, "shew that person to me, Spirit, I beseech you!"

The Phantom spread its dark robe before him for a moment, like a wing; and withdrawing it, revealed a room by daylight, where a mother and her children were.

She was expecting some one, and with anxious eagerness; for she walked up and down the room; started at every sound; looked out from the window; glanced at the clock; tried, but in vain, to work with her needle; and could hardly bear the voices of the children in their play.

At length the knock was heard. She hurried to the door, and met her husband; a man whose face was care-worn and depressed, though he was young. There was a remarkable expression in it now; a kind of serious delight of which he felt ashamed, and which he struggled to repress.

He sat down to the dinner that had been warming for him by the fire; and when she asked him faintly what news, what news,

Oh cold, cold, rigid, dreadful Death, set up thine altar here, and dress it with such terrors as thou hast at thy command; for this is thy dominion. But of the loved, revered, and honored head, thou canst not turn one hair to thy dread purposes, or make one feature odious. It is not that the hand is heavy and will fall down when released; it is not that the heart and pulse are still; but that the hand WAS open, generous, and true; the heart brave, warm, and tender; and the pulse a man's. Strike, Shadow, strike! And see his good deeds springing from the wound, to sow the world with life immortal!

No voice pronounced these words in Scrooge's ears, and yet he heard them, when he looked upon the bed. He thought, if this man could be raised up now, what would be his foremost thoughts? Avarice, hard dealing, griping cares? They have brought him to a rich end, truly!

He lay, in the dark empty house, with not a man, a woman, or a child to say, he was kind to me in this or that and for the memory of one kind word, I will be kind to him. A cat was tearing at the door, and there was a sound of gnawing rats beneath the hearth-stone. What *they* wanted in the room of death, and why they were so restless and disturbed, Scrooge did not dare to think.

"Spirit!" he said, "this is a fearful place. In leaving it, I shall not leave its lesson, trust me. Let us go!"

Still the Ghost pointed, with unmoving finger to the head.

"I understand you," Scrooge returned, "and I would do it, if I could. But I have not the power, Spirit. I have not the power."

Again it seemed to look upon him.

"If there is any person in the town, who feels emotion caused by this man's death," said Scrooge quite agonized, "shew that person to me, Spirit, I beseech you!"

The phantom spread its dark robe before him for a moment, like a wing; and withdrawing it, revealed a room by daylight, where a mother and her children were.

She was expecting some one, and with anxious eagerness; for she walked up and down the room; started at every sound; looked out from the window; glanced at the clock; tried, but in vain, to work with her needle; and could hardly bear the voices of the children in their play.

At length the long-expected knock was heard. She hurried to the door, and met her husband; a man whose face was care-worn and depressed, though he was young. There was a remarkable expression in it now; a kind of serious delight of which he felt ashamed, and which he struggled to repress.

He sat down to the dinner, that had been hoarding for him by the fire; and when she asked him faintly what news, (which was not until after a long silence) appeared embarrassed how to answer.

"Is it good", she said, "or bad?" — to help him.

"Bad," he answered.

"We are quite ruined."

"No. There is hope yet, Caroline."

"If he relents," she said, amazed. "There is! Nothing is past hope, if such a miracle has happened."

"He is past relenting", said her husband. "He is dead."

She was a mild and patient creature if her face spoke truth; but she was thankful in her soul to hear it, and she said so, with clasped hands. She prayed forgiveness the next moment, and was sorry, but the first was the emotion of her heart.

"What the drunken woman whom I told you of last night, said to me, when I tried to see him and obtain a week's delay; and what I thought was a mere excuse to avoid me; turns out to have been quite true. He was not only very ill, but dying, then."

"To whom will our debt be transferred?"

"I don't know. But before that time we shall be ready with the money; and even though we were not, it would be bad fortune indeed to find so merciless a creditor in his successor. We may sleep tonight with light hearts, Caroline!"

Yes. Soften it as they would, their hearts were lighter. The children's faces hushed and clustered round to hear what they so little understood, were brighter; and it was a happier house for this man's death! The only emotion that the Ghost could shew him, caused by the event, was one of pleasure.

"Let me see some tenderness connected with a death", said Scrooge; "or that dark chamber, Spirit, which we left just now, will be for ever present to me."

The Ghost conducted him through several streets familiar to his feet; and as they went along, Scrooge looked here and there to find himself, but nowhere was he to be seen. They entered poor Bob Cratchit's house — the dwelling he had visited before — and found the mother and the children seated round the fire.

Quiet. Very quiet. The noisy little Cratchits were as still as statues in one corner, and sat looking up at Peter, who had a book before him. The mother and her daughters were engaged in sewing. But surely they were very quiet!

"And He took a child, and set him in the midst of them." Where had Scrooge heard those words? He had not dreamed them. The boy must have read them out, as he and the Spirit crossed the threshold. Why did he not go on!

The mother laid her work upon the table, and put her hand up to her face.

"The colour hurts my eyes," she said.

The colour? Ah, poor Tiny Tim!

"They're better now again", said Cratchit's wife. "It makes them (which was not until after a long silence) appeared embarrassed how to answer.

"Is it good?" she said, "or bad?"—to help him.

"Bad," he answered.

"We are quite ruined."

"No. There is hope yet, Caroline."

"If *he* relents," she said, amazed, "there is! Nothing is past hope, if such a miracle has happened."

"He is past relenting," said her husband. "He is dead."

She was a mild and patient creature if her face spoke truth; but she was thankful in her soul to hear it, and she said so, with clasped hands. She prayed forgiveness the next moment, and was sorry, but the first was the emotion of her heart.

"What the half-drunken woman whom I told you of last night, said to me, when I tried to see him and obtain a week's delay; and what I thought was a mere excuse to avoid me; turns out to have been quite true. He was not only very ill, but dying, then."

"To whom will our debt be transferred?"

"I don't know. But before that time we shall be ready with the money; and even though we were not, it would be a bad fortune indeed to find so merciless a creditor in his successor. We may sleep tonight with light hearts, Caroline!"

Yes. Soften it as they would, their hearts were lighter. The children's faces hushed, and clustered round to hear what they so little understood, were brighter; and it was a happier house for this man's death! The only emotion, that the Ghost could show him, caused by the event, was one of pleasure.

"Let me see some tenderness connected with a death," said Scrooge; "or that dark chamber, Spirit, which we left just now, will be for ever present to me."

The Ghost conducted him, through several streets familiar to his feet; and as they went along, Scrooge looked here and there to find himself, but nowhere was he to be seen. They entered poor Bob Cratchit's house—the dwelling he had visited before—and found the mother and the children seated round the fire.

Quiet. Very quiet. The noisy little Cratchits were as still as statues in one corner, and sat looking up at Peter, who had a Book before him. The mother and her daughters were engaged in sewing. But surely they were very quiet!

" 'And He took a child, and set him in the midst of them.' "

Where had Scrooge heard those words? He had not dreamed them. The boy must have read them out, as he and the Spirit crossed the threshhold.

Why did he not go on!

The mother laid her work upon the table, and put her hand up to her face.

"The colour hurts my eyes!" she said.

The colour? Ah poor Tiny Tim!

"They're better now again," said Cratchit's wife. "It makes them

...by candle-light. And I wouldn't show weak eyes to your father when he comes home, for the world. It must be near his time.

"Past it rather," Peter answered, shutting up his book. "But I think he has walked a little slower than he used, these few last evenings, mother."

They were very quiet again. At last she said, and in a steady cheerful voice, that only faltered once: "I have known him walk with — I have known him walk with Tiny Tim upon his shoulder, very fast indeed."

"And so have I," cried Peter. "Often."

"And so have I," exclaimed another. So had all.

"But he was very light to carry," she resumed, intent upon her work, "and his father loved him so, that it was no trouble — no trouble. And there is your father at the door!"

She hurried out to meet him; and little Bob in his comforter — he had need of it, poor fellow — came in. His tea was ready for him on the hob, and they all tried who should help him to it most. Then the two young Cratchits got upon his knees and laid, each child a little cheek, against his face, as if they said, "Don't mind it, father. Don't be grieved!"

Bob was very cheerful with them, and spoke pleasantly to all the family. He looked at the work upon the table, and praised the industry and speed of the girls. They would be done long before Sunday, he said.

"Sunday! You went to-day, then, Robert?" said his wife.

"Yes, my dear," returned Bob. "I wish you could have gone. It would have done you good to see how green a place it is. But you'll see it often. I promised him that I would walk there on a Sunday. My little, little child!" cried Bob. "My little child!"

He broke down all at once. He couldn't help it. If he could have helped it, he and his child would have been farther apart perhaps than they were.

He left the room, and went up stairs into the room above, which was lighted cheerfully, and hung with Christmas. There was a chair set close beside the child, and signs of some one having been there, lately. Poor Bob sat down in it, and when he had thought a little and composed himself, he kissed the little face. He was reconciled to what had happened, and went down again quite happy.

They drew about the fire, and talked; the girls and mother working still. Bob told them of the extraordinary kindness of Mr Scrooge's nephew, whom he had scarcely seen but once, and who, meeting him in the street that day, and weak by candle-light; and I wouldn't shew weak eyes to your father when he comes home, for the world. It must be near his time."

"Past it, rather," Peter answered, shutting up his book. "But I think he's walked a little slower than he used, these few last evenings, mother."

They were very quiet again. At last she said, and in a steady cheerful voice, that only faultered once:

"I have known him walk with—I have known him walk with Tiny Tim upon his shoulder, very fast indeed."

"And so have I," cried Peter. "Often!"

"And so have I!" exclaimed another. So had all.

"But he was very light to carry," she resumed, intent upon her work, "and his father loved him so, that it was no trouble—no trouble. And there *is* your father at the door!"

She hurried out to meet him; and little Bob in his Comforter—he had need of it, poor fellow—came in. His tea was ready for him on the hob, and they all tried who should help him to it most. Then the two young Cratchits, got up on his knees and laid, each child a little cheek, against his face, as if they said, "Don't mind it, father. Don't be grieved!"

Bob was very cheerful with them, and spoke pleasantly to all the family. He looked at the work upon the table, and praised the industry and speed of Mrs. Cratchit and the girls. They would be done long before Sunday he said.

"Sunday! You went today then Robert?" said his wife.

"Yes, my dear," returned Bob. "I wish you could have gone. It would have done you good to see how green a place it is. But you'll see it often. I promised him that I would walk there on a Sunday. My little, little child!" cried Bob. "My little child!"

He broke down all at once. He couldn't help it. If he could have helped it, he and his child would have been farther apart perhaps than they were.

He left the room, and went up stairs into the room above, which was lighted cheerfully, and hung with Christmas. There was a chair set close beside the child, and there were signs of some one having been there, lately. Poor Bob sat down in it, and when he had thought a little and composed himself, he kissed the little face. He was reconciled to what had happened, and went down again quite happy.

They drew about the fire, and talked; the girls and mother working still. Bob told them of the extraordinary kindness of Mr. Scrooge's nephew, whom he had scarcely seen but once, and who, meeting him in the street that day, and seeing that he looked a little, "just a little down you know," said Bob, enquired what had happened to distress him. "on which," said Bob, "for he is the pleasantest-spoken gentleman you ever heard, I told him. 'I am heartily sorry for it, Mr Cratchit' he said, 'and heartily sorry for your good wife. If he ever knew that, I don't know!'"

"Knew what, my dear?"

"Why, that you were a good wife," replied Bob.

"Everybody knows that!" said Peter.

"Well said, my boy!" cried Bob, "I hope they do.—'Heartily sorry,' he said 'for your good wife. If I can be of service to you in any way,' he said, 'that's where I live. Pray come to me.' Now it wasn't," cried Bob, "for the sake of anything he might be able to do for us, so much as for his kind way, that this was quite delightful. It really seemed as if he had known our Tiny Tim, and felt with us!"

"I'm sure he's a good soul!" said Mrs Cratchit.

"You would be surer of it, my dear," returned Bob, "if you saw and spoke to him. I shouldn't be at all surprised, mark what I say, if he got Peter a better situation."

"Only hear that, Peter!" said Mrs Cratchit.

"And then," cried one of the girls, "Peter will be keeping company with some one, and setting up for himself."

"Get along with you!" retorted Peter, grinning.

"It's just as likely as not," said Bob, "one of these days; though there's plenty of time for that, my dear. But however and whenever we part from one another, I am sure we shall none of us forget poor Tiny Tim—shall we—or this first parting that there was among us."

"Never, father!" cried they all.

"And I know," said Bob, "I know, my dears, that when we recollect how patient and how mild he was, although he was a little, little child, we shall not quarrel easily among ourselves, and forget poor Tiny Tim in doing it."

"No, never, father!" they all cried again.

"I am very happy," said little Bob, "I am very happy!"

Mrs Cratchit kissed him, his daughters kissed him, the two young Cratchits kissed him, and Peter and himself shook hands. Spirit of Tiny Tim, thy childish essence was from God!

"Spectre," said Scrooge, "something informs me that our parting moment is at hand. I know it, but I know not how. Tell me what man that was whom we saw lying dead?"

The Ghost of Christmas Yet To Come conveyed him, as before—though at a different time, he thought: indeed, there seemed no order in these latter visions, save that they were in the Future—into the resorts of business men, but showed him not himself. Indeed, the Spirit did not stay for anything, but went straight on, as to seeing that he looked a little—"just a little down you know," said Bob—enquired what had happened to distress him. "On which," said Bob; "for he is the pleasantest-spoken gentleman you ever heard, I told him. 'I am heartily sorry for it, Mr. Cratchit' he said, 'and heartily sorry for your good wife.' By the bye, how he ever knew *that*, I don't know!"

"Knew what, my dear?"

"Why, that you were a good wife," replied Bob.

"Everybody knows that!" said Peter.

"Very well observed my boy!" cried Bob. "I hope they do. —'Heartily sorry,' he said, 'for your good wife. If I can be of service to you in any way,' he said, giving me his card, 'that's where I live. Pray come to me.' Now, it wasn't," cried Bob, "for the sake of anything he might be able to do for us, so much as for his kind way, that this was quite delightful. It really seemed as if he had known our Tiny Tim, and felt with us!"

"I'm sure he's a good soul!" said Mrs. Cratchit.

"You would be surer of it, my dear," returned Bob, "if you saw and spoke to him. I shouldn't be at all surprised; mark what I say; if he got Peter a better situation."

"Only hear that, Peter!" said Mrs. Cratchit.

"And then," cried one of the girls, "Peter will be keeping company with some one, and setting up for himself."

"Get along with you!" retorted Peter, grinning.

"It's just as likely as not," said Bob, "one of these days; though there's plenty of time for that, my dear. But however and whenever we part from one another, I am sure we shall none of us forget poor Tiny Tim—shall we—or this first parting that there was among us."

"Never, father!" cried they all.

"And I know," said Bob, "I know, my dears, that when we recollect how patient and how mild he was; although he was a little, little child, we shall not quarrel easily among ourselves, and forget poor Tiny Tim in doing it."

"No, never father!" they all cried again.

"I am very happy," said little Bob, "I am very happy."

Mrs. Cratchit kissed him, his daughters kissed him, the two young Cratchits kissed him, and Peter and himself shook hands. Spirit of Tiny Tim, thy childish essence was from God!

"Spectre!" said Scrooge, "Something informs me that our parting-moment is at hand. I know it, but I know not how. Tell me what man that was whom we saw lying dead."

The Ghost of Christmas Yet To Come conveyed him, as before (though at a different time, he thought; indeed, there seemed no order in these latter visions, save that they were in the Future) into the resorts of business men, but shewed him not himself. Indeed, the Spirit did not stay for anything, but went straight on as to

this end depend ... just so non desired,
... ~~~ besought by Scrooge to tarry for a moment.

"This court," said Scrooge, "through which we hurry now, is where my place of occupation is, and has been for a length of time. ... but we behold what I shall be, in days to come."

The Spirit stopped; but the hand was not pointed ... elsewhere, ...
... "The house is yonder," Scrooge exclaimed. "Why do you point away?"

The ... finger underwent no change. Scrooge ... to the window of his office, and looked at it. It was an office still, ... dark ... but not his. The furniture was not the same, and the figure in the ... was not himself. The phantom pointed as before.

Scrooge joined it once again, and wondering ... it, until they reached an iron gate. He paused to look ... before entering.

A churchyard! Here then, the wretched man ... It was a worthy place. Walled in by houses ... of vegetation's death: not life. Choked up with too much burying ... reflected appetite. A worthy place!

The Spirit stood among the graves, and ... pointed down to One. He advanced ... towards it trembling. The phantom was exactly as it had been, but he dreaded that he saw new meaning in its solemn shape.

"Before I draw nearer to that stone to which you point," said Scrooge, "... one question. Are these the shadows of the things that Will be, or are they shadows of the things that ... be, only."

The Spirit pointed downward to the grave by which it stood.

"Men's courses will foreshadow ... certain ends, to which, if persevered in, they must lead," said Scrooge. "But if the courses be departed from, the ends will change. Say it is thus with what you show me!"

The Spirit was unmovable as ever.

Scrooge crept towards it, trembling as he went; and following the finger, read upon the stone of the neglected grave, his own name, Ebenezer Scrooge.

"Am I that man who lay upon the bed?" he cried, upon his knees. The finger pointed from the grave to him, and back again.

"No, Spirit! oh no, no!"

The finger still was there.

"Spirit!" he cried, tight clutching at its robe. "Hear me! I am not the man I was. I will not be the man I must have been, ... Why show me this, if I am past all hope!"

the end just now desired, until besought by Scrooge to tarry for a moment.

"This court," said Scrooge, "through which we hurry now, is where my place of occupation is, and has been for a length of time. I see the house. Let me behold what I shall be, in days to come."

The Spirit stopped; the hand was pointed elsewhere.

"The house is yonder," Scrooge exclaimed. "Why do you point away?"

The inexorable finger underwent no change.

Scrooge hastened to the window of his office, and looked in. It was an office still, but not his. The furniture was not the same, and the figure in the chair was not himself. The phantom pointed as before.

He joined it once again, and wondering why and whither he had gone, accompanied it, until they reached an iron gate. He paused to look round, before entering.

A churchyard! Here, then, the wretched man whose name he had now to learn, lay underneath the ground. It was a worthy place. Walled in by houses. Overrun by grass and weeds, the growth of vegetation's death: not life. Choked up with too much burying. Fat with repleted appetite. A worthy place indeed!

The Spirit stood among the graves, and pointed down to One. He advanced towards it trembling. The phantom was exactly as it had been, but he dreaded that he saw new meaning in its solemn shape.

"Before I draw nearer to that stone to which you point," said Scrooge, "answer me one question. Are these the shadows of the things that Will be, or are they shadows of things that May be, only."

Still the Ghost pointed downward to the grave by which it stood.

"Mens' courses will foreshadow certain ends to which, if persevered in, they must lead," said Scrooge. "But if the courses be departed from, the ends will change. Say it is thus, with what you shew me!"

The Spirit was immovable as ever.

Scrooge crept towards it, trembling as he went; and following the finger, read upon the stone of the neglected grave, his own name EBENEZER SCROOGE.

"Am *I* that man who lay upon the bed!" he cried, upon his knees.

The finger pointed from the grave to him, and back again.

"No Spirit! Oh no, no!"

The finger still was there.

"Spirit!" he cried, tight clutching at its robe. "Hear me! I am not the man I was. I will not be the man I must have been, but for this intercourse. Why shew me this, if I am past all hope!"

60

For the first time, the hand appeared to shake.

"Good Spirit," he pursued, as down upon the ground he ~~[crossed out]~~ fell before it. "Your nature intercedes for me, and pities me. Assure me that I yet may change these shadows you have shewn me, by an altered life!"

The kind hand trembled.

"I will honour Christmas in my heart, and try to keep it all the year. I will live in the Past, the Present, and the Future. The Spirits of all Three shall strive within me. I will not shut out the lessons that they teach. Oh, tell me I may ~~sponge away~~ the writing on this stone!"

In his agony, he caught the ~~[crossed out]~~ spectral hand. It sought to free itself, but he was strong in his entreaty, and detained it. The Spirit, stronger yet, repulsed him.

Holding up his hands in one last prayer to have his fate reversed, he saw ~~[crossed out]~~ an alteration in the phantom's hood and dress. It ~~[crossed out]~~ shrunk, ~~[crossed out]~~ collapsed, ~~[crossed out]~~ and dwindled down into a bedpost.

For the first time the hand appeared to shake.

"Good Spirit," he pursued, as down upon the ground he fell before it. "Your nature intercedes for me, and pities me. Assure me that I yet may change these shadows you have shewn me, by an altered life!"

The kind hand trembled.

"I will honour Christmas in my heart, and try to keep it all the year. I will live in the Past, the Present, and the Future. The Spirits of all Three shall strive within me. I will not shut out the lessons that they teach. Oh tell me, I may sponge away the writing on this stone!"

In his agony, he caught the spectral hand. It sought to free itself, but he was strong in his entreaty, and detained it. The Spirit, stronger yet, repulsed him.

Holding up his hands in one last prayer to have his fate reversed, he saw an alteration in the phantom's hood and dress. It shrunk, collapsed, and dwindled down into a bedpost.

61

Stave V.

The end of it.

Yes! and the bedpost was his own. The bed was his own, the room was his own. Best and happiest of all, the Time before him was his own, to make amends in!

"I will live in the Past, the Present, and the Future!" Scrooge repeated, as he scrambled out of bed. "The Spirits of all Three shall strive within me. Oh Jacob Marley, and the Christmas time be praised for this! I say it on my knees, old Jacob, on my knees!"

He was so fluttered and so glowing with his good intentions that his broken voice would scarcely answer to his call. He had been sobbing violently in his conflict with the Spirit, and his face was wet with tears.

"They are not torn down," cried Scrooge, folding one of his curtains in his arms, "they are not torn down, rings and all. They are here — I am here — the shadows of the things that would have been, may be dispelled. They will be. I know they will!"

His hands were busy with his garments all this time; turning them inside out, putting them on upside down, tearing them, mislaying them, making them parties to every kind of extravagance.

"I don't know what to do!" cried Scrooge, laughing and crying in the same breath. "I am as light as a feather, I am as happy as an angel, I am as merry as a schoolboy. I am as giddy as a drunken man. Whoop! Hallo here! Hoop! A merry Christmas to everybody! A happy New Year to all the world. Hallo here! Whoop! Hallo!"

He had frisked into the sitting-room and was now standing there: perfectly winded.

"There's the saucepan that the gruel was in!" cried Scrooge, starting off again, and frisking round the fireplace. "There's the door by which the Ghost of Jacob Marley entered! There's the corner where the Ghost of Christmas Present sat! There's the window where I saw the wandering Spirits! It's all right, it's all true, it all happened. Ha ha ha!"

Really, for a man who had been out of practice for so many years, it was a splendid laugh, a most illustrious laugh. The father of a long, long line of brilliant laughs!

"I don't know what day of the month it is!" said Scrooge. "I don't know how long I've been among the Spirits. I don't know anything. I'm quite a baby. Never mind. I don't care. I'd rather be a baby. Hallo! Whoop! Hallo here!"

STAVE V.

The End of It.

Yes! And the bedpost was his own. The bed was his own, the room was his own. Best and happiest of all, the Time before him was his own, to make amends in!

"I will live in the Past, the Present, and the Future!" Scrooge repeated, as he scrambled out of bed. "The Spirits of all Three shall strive within me. Oh Jacob Marley, Heaven, and the Christmas Time be praised for this! I say it on my knees, old Jacob; on my knees!"

He was so fluttered and so glowing with his good intentions, that his broken voice would scarcely answer to his call. He had been sobbing violently in his conflict with the Spirit and his face was wet with tears.

"They are not torn down," cried Scrooge, folding one of his bed-curtains in his arms, "they are not torn down, rings and all. They are here; I am here; the shadows of the things that would have been, may be dispelled. They will be. I know they will!"

His hands were busy with his garments all this time: turning them inside out, putting them on upside down, tearing them, losing them, playing at ball with them: making them parties to every kind of extravagance.

"I don't know what to do!" cried Scrooge, laughing and crying in the same breath. "I am as light as a feather, I am as happy as an angel. I am as merry as a schoolboy. I am as giddy as a drunken man. Whoop! Hallo there! Hoop! A Merry Christmas to everybody! A happy New Year to all the world. Hallo here! Hoop! Hallo!"

He had frisked into the sitting-room, and was now standing on one leg: perfectly winded.

"There's the saucepan that the gruel was in!" cried Scrooge, starting off again, and frisking round the fireplace. "There's the door by which the Ghost of Jacob Marley entered! There's the corner where the Ghost of Christmas Present sat! There's the window where I saw the wandering Spirits! It's all right, it's all fine, it all happened. Ha ha ha!"

Really, for a man who had been out of practice for so many years, it was a splendid laugh, a most illustrious laugh. The father of a long, long, line of brilliant laughs!

"I don't know what day of the month it is!" said Scrooge. "I don't know how long I've been among the Spirits. I don't know anything. I'm quite a baby. Never mind. I don't care. I'd rather be a baby. Hallo! Whoop! Hallo here!"

62

He was checked in his transports by the churches ringing out the lustiest peals he had ever heard. Clash, clang, hammer, ding, dong, bell; bell, dong, ding, hammer, clang, clash. Glorious, glorious!

Running to the window, he opened it, and put out his head. No fog, no mist; clear, bright, jovial, stirring, cold; cold, piping for the blood to dance to — Golden sunlight; Heavenly sky; sweet fresh air; merry bells. Oh, glorious, glorious!

"What's to day!" cried Scrooge, calling downward to a boy in Sunday clothes, who perhaps had loitered in to look about him.

"Eh?" returned the boy, with all his might of wonder.

"What's to day, my fine fellow!" said Scrooge.

"To day!" replied the boy. "Why, Christmas Day!"

"It's Christmas Day!" said Scrooge to himself. "I haven't missed it. The Spirits have done it all in one night. They can do anything they like. Of course they can. Of course they can. Hallo my fine fellow!"

"Hallo!" returned the boy.

"Do you know the Poulterer's in the next street but one, at the corner?" Scrooge enquired.

"I should hope I did," replied the lad.

"An intelligent boy!" said Scrooge. "A remarkable boy! Do you know whether they've sold the prize turkey that was hanging up there; not the little prize turkey, the big one."

"What, the one as big as me!" returned the boy.

"What a delightful boy!" said Scrooge. "It's a pleasure to talk to him. Yes, my buck!"

"It's hanging there now," replied the boy.

"Is it?" said Scrooge. "Go and buy it."

"Walk-ER!" exclaimed the boy.

"No, no," said Scrooge. "I am in earnest. Go and buy it, and tell 'em to bring it here, that I may give 'em the direction where to take it. Come back with the man, and I'll give you a shilling. Come back with him in less than five minutes, and I'll give you half a crown!"

The boy was off like a shot. He must have had a steady hand at a trigger who could have got a shot off half so fast.

"I'll send it to Bob Cratchit's!" whispered Scrooge, rubbing his hands, and splitting with a laugh. "He shan't know who sends it. It's twice the size of Tiny Tim. Joe Miller never made such a joke as sending it to Bob's will be!"

He was checked in his transports by the churches ringing out the lustiest peals he had ever heard. Clash, clang, hammer, ding, dong, bell: bell, dong, ding, hammer, clang, clash! Oh glorious, glorious!

Running to the window, he opened it, and put out his head. No fog, no mist. Clear, bright, jovial, stirring, cold—cold, piping for the blood to dance to—golden sunlight; Heavenly sky; sweet fresh air; merry bells—oh glorious, glorious!

"What's to day?" cried Scrooge, calling downward to a boy in Sunday clothes, who perhaps had loitered in to look about him.

"EH?" returned the boy, with all his might of wonder.

"What's to day, my fine fellow!" said Scrooge.

"Today!" replied the boy. "Why, CHRISTMAS DAY!"

"It's Christmas Day!" said Scrooge to himself. "I haven't missed it. The Spirits, have done it all in one night. They can do anything they like. Of course they can. Of course they can. Hallo my fine fellow!"

"Hallo!" returned the boy.

"Do you know the Poulterer's in the next street but one, at the corner?" Scrooge inquired.

"I should hope I did," replied the lad.

"An intelligent boy!" said Scrooge. "A remarkable boy! Do you know whether they've sold the prize Turkey that was hanging up there; not the little prize turkey, the big one?"

"What, the one as big as me!" returned the boy.

"What a delightful boy!" said Scrooge. "It's a pleasure to talk to him. Yes, my buck!"

"It's hanging there now," replied the boy.

"Is it?" said Scrooge. "Go and buy it."

"Walk-ER!" exclaimed the boy.

"No, no," said Scrooge, "I am in earnest. Go and buy it, and tell 'em to bring it here, that I may give 'em the direction where to take it. Come back with the man, and I'll give you a shilling. Come back with him in less than five minutes, and I'll give you half a crown!"

The boy was off like a shot. He must have had a steady hand at a trigger who could have got a shot off half so fast.

"I'll send it to Bob Cratchit's!" whispered Scrooge, rubbing his hands, and splitting with a laugh. "He shan't know who sends it. It's twice the size of Tiny Tim. Joe Miller never made such a joke as sending it to Bob's will be!"

The hand in which he wrote the address, was not a steady one, but write it he did. somehow, and went down stairs to open the street door, ready for the coming of the Poulterer's man. as he stood there, awaiting his arrival, the knocker caught his eye.

"I shall love it, as long as I live!" cried Scrooge, patting it with his hand. "I scarcely ever looked at it before. what an honest expression it has in its face! It's a wonderful knocker! —Here's the turkey. Hallo! whoop! How are you! merry christmas!"

It was a Turkey! He never could have stood upon his legs, that bird. He would have snapped 'em short off, in a minute, like sticks of sealing wax.

"why, it's impossible to carry that to camden Town," said Scrooge. "You must have a cab."

The chuckle with which he said this, and the chuckle with which he paid for the cab, and the chuckle with which he recompensed the boy, were only exceeded by the chuckle with which he sat down breathless in his chair again, and chuckled 'till he cried.

Shaving was not an easy task, for his hand continued to shake very much; and shaving requires attention, even when you don't dance while you are at it. But if he had cut the end of his nose off, he would have put a piece of sticking-plaister over it, and been quite satisfied.

He dressed himself "all in his best," and at last got out into the streets. The people were by this time pouring forth, as he had seen them with the Ghost of christmas Present; and walking with his hands behind him, Scrooge regarded everyone with a delighted smile. He looked so irresistibly pleasant, in a word, that three or four good-humoured fellows said "Good morning sir! a merry christmas to you!" And Scrooge said often afterwards that of all the blithe sounds he had ever heard, those were the blithest in his ears.

He had not gone far, when coming on towards him he beheld the portly gentleman who had walked into his counting house the day before, and said "Scrooge and Marley's I believe?" It sent a pang across his heart to think how this old gentleman would look upon him when they met; but he knew what path lay straight before him, and he took it.

"My dear sir," said Scrooge, quickening his pace, and taking the old gentleman by both his hands. "How do you do? I hope you succeeded yesterday. It was very kind of you. a merry christmas to you Sir!"

"Mr Scrooge!"

"Yes," said Scrooge. "That is my name, and I fear it may not be pleasant to you. Allow me to ask your pardon. and will you have the goodness—" here Scrooge whispered in his ear.

"Lord bless me!" cried the gentleman, as if his breath were gone. "My dear

The hand in which he wrote the address, was not a steady one, but write it he did, somehow, and went down stairs to open the street door, ready for the coming of the Poulterer's man. As he stood there, waiting his arrival, the knocker caught his eye.

"I shall love it, as long as I live!" cried Scrooge, patting it with his hand. "I scarcely ever looked at it before. What an honest expression it has in its face! It's a wonderful knocker!—Here's the turkey. Hallo! Whoop! How are you! Merry Christmas!"

It *was* a Turkey! He never could have stood upon his legs, that bird. He would have snapped 'em short off, in a minute, like sticks of sealing wax.

"Why, it's impossible to carry that to Camden Town," said Scrooge. "You must have a cab."

The chuckle with which he said this, and the chuckle with which he paid for the Turkey, and the chuckle with which he paid for the cab, and the chuckle with which he recompensed the boy, were only to be exceeded by the chuckle with which he sat down breathless on his chair again, and chuckled 'till he cried.

Shaving was not an easy task, for his hand continued to shake very much; and shaving requires attention, even when you don't dance while you are at it. But if he had cut the end of his nose off, he would have put a piece of sticking-plaister over it, and been quite satisfied.

He dressed himself "all in his best," and at last got out into the streets. The people were by this time pouring forth, as he had seen them with the Ghost of Christmas Present; and walking with his hands behind him Scrooge regarded everyone with a delighted smile. He looked so irresistibly pleasant, in a word, that three or four good-humoured fellows said "Good morning Sir! A merry Christmas to you!" And Scrooge said often afterwards that of all the blithe sounds he had ever heard, these were the blithest in his ears.

He had not gone far, when coming on towards him he beheld the portly gentleman who had walked into his counting house the day before, and said "Scrooge and Marley's I believe?" It sent a pang across his heart to think how this old gentleman would look upon him when they met; but he knew what path lay straight before him, and he took it.

"My Dear Sir," said Scrooge, quickening his pace, and taking the old gentleman by both his hands. "How do you do? I hope you succeeded yesterday. It was very kind of you. A merry Christmas to you Sir!"

"Mr. Scrooge!"

"Yes," said Scrooge, "that's my name, and I fear it may not be pleasant to you. Allow me to ask your pardon. And will you have the goodness—" here Scrooge whispered in his ear.

"Lord bless me!" cried the gentleman, as if his breath were gone. "My dear the Scrooge, all you sorrows?"

"If you please," said Scrooge. "Not a farthing less. A great many back-payments are included in it, I assure you. Will you do me that favor?"

"My dear sir!" said the other, shaking hands with him again. "I don't know what to say to such munifi—"

"Don't say anything, please," retorted Scrooge. "Come and see me. Will you come and see me?"

"I will!" cried the old gentleman. And it was clear he meant to do it.

"Thankee," said Scrooge. "I am much obliged to you. I thank you fifty times. Bless you!"

He went to church, and walked about the streets, and watched the people hurrying to and fro, and looked down into the kitchens of houses, and up to the windows; and found that everything could yield him pleasure. He had never dreamed that any walk—that anything—could give him so much happiness. In the afternoon he turned his steps towards his nephew's house.

He passed the door a dozen times, before he had the courage to go up and knock. But he made a dash, and did it:

"Is your master at home, my dear?" said Scrooge to the girl.

"Yes sir."

"Where is he, my love?" said Scrooge.

"He's in the dining-room, sir, along with mistress. I'll shew you up, if you please."

"He knows me," said Scrooge, with his hand already on the dining-room lock. "I'll go in here, my dear."

He turned it gently, and sidled his face in, round the door. They were looking at the table (which was spread out in great array;) for these young housekeepers are always nervous on such points, and like to see that everything is right.

"Fred!" said Scrooge.

How his niece by marriage started! Scrooge had forgotten, for the moment, about her sitting in the corner with the footstool, or he wouldn't have done it, on any account.

"Why, bless my soul!" cried Fred, "who's that?"

"Your uncle Scrooge. I have come to dinner. Will you let me in, Fred?"

Let him in! It is a mercy he didn't shake his arm off. He was at home in five minutes. Nothing could be heartier. His niece looked just the same. So did Topper, did the plump sister, when she came. So did every one when they came. Wonderful party, wonderful games, wonderful

Mr. Scrooge, are you serious?"

"If you please," said Scrooge. "Not a farthing less. A great many back-payments are included in it, I assure you. Will you do me that favor?"

"My dear sir!" cried the other, shaking hands with him again. "I don't know what to say to such munifi—"

"Don't say anything, please," retorted Scrooge. "Come and see me. Will you come and see me?"

"I will!" cried the old gentleman. And it was clear he meant to do it.

"Thank'ee," said Scrooge. "I am much obliged to you. I thank you fifty times. God bless you!"

He went to church and walked about the streets, and watched the people hurrying to and fro, and patted children on the head, and questioned beggars, and looked down into the kitchens of houses, and up to the windows; and found that anything could yield him pleasure. He had never dreamed that any walk—that anything—could give him so much happiness. In the afternoon he turned his steps towards his nephew's house.

He passed the door a dozen times, before he had the courage to go up and knock. But he made a dash, and did it:

"Is your master at home my dear?" said Scrooge to the girl. Nice girl! Very.

"Yes Sir."

"Where is he my love?" said Scrooge.

"He's in the dining-room Sir, along with mistress. I'll shew you upstairs, if you please."

"Thank'ee. He knows me," said Scrooge, with his hand already on the dining-room lock. "I'll go in here, my dear."

He turned it gently, and sidled his face in, round the door. They were looking at the table (which was spread out in great array); for these young housekeepers are always nervous on such points, and like to see that everything is right.

"Fred!" said Scrooge.

Dear heart alive, how his niece by marriage, started! Scrooge had forgotten for the moment, about her sitting in the corner with the footstool, or he wouldn't have done it, on any account.

"Why bless my soul!" cried Fred, "who's that?"

"It's I. Your uncle Scrooge. I have come to dinner. Will you let me in, Fred?"

Let him in! It is a mercy he didn't shake his arm off. He was at home in five minutes. Nothing could be heartier. His niece looked just the same. So did Topper, when *he* came. So did the plump sister, when *she* came. So did every one when they came. Wonderful party, wonderful games, wonderful unanimity ^won-der-ful happiness!

But he was ^at the office next morning, oh he was ^there ▲ If he could only catch ^Bob Cratchit coming late! That was the thing he had set ^upon his heart upon.

And he did it; Yes he did! The clock struck nine. No Bob. a quarter past. no Bob. It was full eighteen minutes and a half, behind his time. Scrooge sat ^with his door wide open, that he ^might see him come into the Tank.

His hat was off, before he opened the door. his comforter too. He was on his stool in a jiffy; driving away with his pen. as if he were trying to outstrip nine o'clock.

"Hullo!" growled Scrooge, in his accustomed voice, as near as he could feign it. "what do you mean by coming ^here at this time of day?"

"I'm very sorry sir"; said Bob. "I am behind my time."

"You are?" repeated Scrooge. "Yes. I think you are. Step this way, if you please."

"It's only once a year sir"; pleaded Bob, appearing from ^the Tank. "It shall not be repeated. I was making rather merry yesterday Sir."

"Now, I'll tell you what, my friend"; said Scrooge. "I am not going to ^stand this sort of thing any longer. And therefore "he continued, leaping from his stool, and giving Bob such a dig in the waistcoat that he staggered back into the Tank again. "and therefore I am about to raise your salary!"

Bob trembled, and got a little nearer to the ruler. He had a ^momentary idea of knocking Scrooge down with it; ^holding him; and calling to the people in the court for help and a Strait Waistcoat.

"A merry Christmas ^Bob," said Scrooge clapping him on the back. "a merrier Christmas ^Bob than I have given you, for many a year! I'll raise your salary, and endeavour to assist your ^struggling family, and we'll ^ discuss your affairs this very afternoon, over a christmas bowl of smoking Bishop, ^Bob! make up the fires and buy another coal scuttle before you dot another i, Bob Cratchit!"

Scrooge was better than his word. He did it all, and infinitely more. ^ as good a friend, as good a master, and as good a man, as the good old city knew, or any other good old ^city, town, or borough, in the good old world. Some people laughed to see the alteration in him, but he let them laugh, and little heeded them; for he was wise enough to know that nothing ever happened on this Globe, for good, at which some people did not have their fill of laughter; and knowing unanimity, won-der-ful happiness!

But he was early at the office next morning. Oh he was early there. If he could only be there first, and catch Bob Cratchit coming late! That was the thing he had set his heart upon.

And he did it; Yes he did! The clock struck nine. No Bob. A quarter past. No Bob. He was full eighteen minutes and a half, behind his time. Scrooge sat with his door wide open, that he might see him come into the Tank.

His hat was off, before he opened the door; his comforter too. He was on his stool in a jiffy: driving away with his pen, as if he were trying to overtake nine o'clock.

"Hullo!" growled Scrooge in his accustomed voice, as near as he could feign it. "What do you mean by coming here at this time of day?"

"I am very sorry Sir," said Bob. "I *am* behind my time."

"You are?" repeated Scrooge. "Yes. I think you are. Step this way, if you please."

"It's only once a year Sir," pleaded Bob, appearing from the Tank. "It shall not be repeated. I was making rather merry, yesterday Sir."

"Now, I'll tell you what, my friend," said Scrooge. "I am not going to stand this sort of thing any longer. And therefore," he continued, leaping from his stool, and giving Bob such a dig in the waistcoat that he staggered back into the Tank again. "And therefore I am about to raise your salary!"

Bob trembled, and got a little nearer to the ruler. He had a momentary idea of knocking Scrooge down with it; holding him; and calling to the people in the court for Help and a Strait Waistcoat.

"A merry Christmas Bob!" said Scrooge with an earnestness that could not be mistaken, as he clapped him on the back. "A merrier Christmas, Bob, than I have given you, for many a year! I'll raise your salary and endeavour to assist your struggling family, and we will discuss your affairs this very afternoon before this very fire, over a Christmas bowl of smoking Bishop, Bob! Make up the fires, and buy another coal-scuttle before you dot another i, Bob Cratchit!"

Scrooge was better than his word. He did it all, and infinitely more.* He became as good a friend, as good a master, and as good a man, as the good old city knew, or any other good old city, town, or borough, in the good old world. Some people laughed to see the alteration in him, but he let them laugh, and little heeded them; for he was wise enough to know that nothing ever happened on this globe, for good, at which some people did not have their fill of laughter in the outset; and knowing

---

* [*Editor's note: in the published version, Dickens inserted here:* and to Tiny Tim, who did NOT die, he was a second father.]

anyway, he thought it quite as well that they should wrinkle up their eyes in grins, as have the malady in *less attractive* forms. His own heart laughed; and that was quite enough for him.

He had no further intercourse with Spirits, but lived upon the Total Abstinence Principle, ever afterwards; and it was always said of him that he knew how to keep Christmas well, if any man alive possessed the knowledge. May that be truly said of us, and all of us! And so, as Tiny Tim observed, God Bless Us, Every One!

The End.
= = =

that such as these would be blind anyway, he thought it quite as well that they should wrinkle up their eyes in grins, as have the malady in less attractive forms. His own heart laughed, and that was quite enough for him.

He had no further intercourse with Spirits, but lived upon the Total Abstinence Principle, ever afterwards; and it was always said of him that he knew how to keep Christmas well, if any man alive possessed the knowledge. May that be truly said of us, and all of us! And so, as Tiny Tim observed, God Bless Us Every One!

THE END.

Acknowledgments

Digital photography of Charles Dickens's original manuscript was generously underwritten by Fay and Geoffrey Elliott.

Many colleagues and friends helped with the preparation of this book, and I am greatly indebted to the following for their assistance: Colin B. Bailey, Karen Banks, Remy Cawley, Graham Haber, Mim Harrison, Joan Kiely, Anna Mageras, Christina Lee Padden, Marilyn Palmeri, Nancy Palmquist, Michael Slater, Reba Snyder, Kristina Stillman, Frank Trujillo, and Matt Weiland.

DK

About the Morgan Library & Museum

A complex of buildings in the heart of New York City, the Morgan Library &
Museum began as the private library of the financier Pierpont Morgan, one
of the preeminent collectors and cultural benefactors in U.S. history. Today it
is a museum, independent research library, musical venue, architectural land-
mark, and historic site. A century after its founding, the Morgan maintains a
unique position in the cultural life of New York City and is considered one of
its greatest treasures. With the 2006 reopening of its newly renovated campus,
designed by the renowned architect Renzo Piano, and the 2010 refurbishment
of the original library, the Morgan reaffirmed its role as an important reposi-
tory for the history, art, and literature of Western civilization from 4000 B.C.E.
to the twenty-first century.

Works by Charles Dickens constitute a particular strength of the Morgan's
celebrated collection of autograph manuscripts. In addition to the original
manuscript of *A Christmas Carol*, the Morgan holds the manuscripts of two
later Christmas books—*The Cricket on the Hearth* (1845) and *The Battle of
Life* (1846)—as well as the entire manuscript and working outlines of Dickens's last completed novel, *Our Mutual Friend* (1864–65). Along with personal
artifacts and photographs of Dickens, the Morgan has more than 1,400 of
his letters.